CRITICAL A

"In *UP FRONT*, Ken Rivard co
flash fiction form. These pieces contain his characteristic
inventions and truths woven together into a wide variety of
vividly drawn characters. The plot of each keeps the reader
off-kilter just enough but in a good way. Each piece is linked
by an up front voice. That voice can be the imaginative
(or not) voice of the teacher, but it is also the voice of the
adult world, and, of course, the adolescent voice. Although
most of the pieces are limited in length, we get to know
these characters and their situations better than we often do
in much longer stories. Rivard conveys his perspective with
complexity, authenticity, compassion, sensitivity and care.
There is a truth and honesty in the writing that will keep you
reading story after story. Rivard proves again that flash fiction
contains much power and depth."

— Robert Hilles, Governor General's Award Winner and
recent author of *Don't Hang Your Soul on That, From
God's Angle,* and *The Pink Puppet*

canalWATCH
(FLASH FICTION, 2022)

"Ken Rivard's mastery of flash fiction is well established.
To get so much juice out of such a tight form is very tricky and
the author is not only concise, but precise in his observations.
He is showing the rest of us louts how to write prose; he's
never lost his poetic touch or let go of his poetic leash,
its telegraphic reach."

— Richard Stevenson (1952–2023), educator and author of
more than 40 books of poetry, haiku and fiction

"Ken Rivard's engaging, thoughtful and at times brilliant collection of flash fiction reveals pain, joy, vulnerability and tenderly observed moments of fleeting life."

— *Alberta Views Magazine*

MOTHERWILD
(NOVEL, 2014)

"In his 10th book, Ken Rivard shows himself to be a pro at capturing the realities of working-class humanity. *Motherwild* is a work of beauty, a coming-of-age story and the eventual healing of a mother-son relationship. Rivard's writing is honest, refreshing, startling, imaginative and gets the reader emotionally involved. *Motherwild* is a really good read!"

— W.P. Kinsella

"Any reader who has gone through life with an addicted family member will relate to the struggles faced by Joey... this is a beautiful book that is sure to tug at the heartstrings of readers everywhere."

— Lisa MacLean, *Tofts Reviews*

"Unique sense of time and place...which [Ken] largely presents without the rose-coloured hue of nostalgia."

— Eric Volmers, *Calgary Herald*

"I enjoyed Motherwild a great deal and I wish you all the success you deserve."

— Denys Arcand, Filmmaker

MISSIONARY POSITIONS
(FICTION, 2008)

"Developing different protagonists with distinct voices is tough but Rivard pulls it off. A master of imagery ... once again Rivard treats these very personal subjects with humanity. *Missionary Positions* reads real, touches readers deeply and hits home on many fronts."

— Wendy Rajala, *Calgary Herald*

WHISKEY EYES
(FICTION, 2004)
Finalist for the Writers' Guild of Alberta Short Fiction Award

"Rivard's flash fiction works ... inventive ... poetic ... all relate to a single narrative arc and thus creating a moving and lasting impression. In an era when more and more people live to an advanced age, many readers are likely to relate to [the main protagonist's] dilemma and find the subtlety and humanity with which Rivard treats this very personal yet universal theme to be a source of comfort and inspiration."

— K. Gordon Neufeld, *Calgary Herald*

"An intense book that deals with the substantial emotional involvement stemming from the responsibility of caring for aging parents."

— Jennifer Partridge, *Calgary Herald*

"Demonstrates the problem when those aged parents become the children ... a difficult problem handled brilliantly.

— Kirk Layton, *Chapters/Indigo Website*

BOTTLE TALK
(FICTION, 2002)
Finalist for the Writers' Guild of Alberta Short Fiction Award

"An excellent display of Rivard's talent as a writer. It is dynamic and sincere and although it is connected by a common thread of alcoholism, the ugly truths that Rivard forces us to view with eyes wide open, are not just those of alcoholism but the basic truths of humanity and life."

— Heather Doody, *Candian Book Review Annual*

"Intensely written with compelling, graphic honesty, Rivard is an astute observer. Reading this book is like probing an open wound that has not healed. It is a brilliant collection of truth and glimpses into one's very soul."

— Anne Burke, *Prairie Journal of Canadian Literature*

MOM, THE SCHOOL FLOODED
(CHILDREN'S LITERATURE, 1995, 2007)

"The book's success is based on its perfect marriage of text and illustration. Ken Rivard's closing dialogue involves the reader in the creative process providing firsthand experience of creative storytelling."

— Christine Linge, *CM Magazine*

"Young readers will enjoy watching someone else test the boundaries of credibility."

— Diane Fitzgerald, *CM Magazine*

"Readers are left with a brilliant illustration to let their minds solve the rest of the story and is an excellent story to add to your collection."

— John Dryden, *CM Magazine*

"A remarkable story about a school gone wet."

— Katherine Garber, *SMS Book Reviews*

SKIN TESTS
(FICTION, 2000)
*Finalist for the Writers' Guild of Alberta Short Fiction Award
and The City of Calgary W.O. Mitchell Book Prize*

IF SHE COULD TAKE ALL THESE MEN
(FICTION, 1995)
Finalist for The Writers' Guild of Alberta Short Fiction Award

"Amazing collection ... captures a poignant vignette from the life of an extraordinary ordinary person. Such thought-provoking portraits bring alive a diverse representation of humanity and render the reader party to intense moments in private lives ... does an absorbing and competent job of conjuring entire lives in these micro-bites of narrative.

— Virginia Gillham, *Canadian Book Review Annual*

"The pleasure is opening one door after another onto lives quickly drawn, sketches of characters caught in odd moments neither random nor monumental. It is this interpretation of lives, this ever-latent potential for changing places, that I find the most engaging quality of this collection, though adroit descriptions are another. The reader will be drawn in by curiosity as to what or who might appear next ... exemplary ... funny... mysterious ... quite wonderful."

— Roo Borson, *Books in Canada*

"Exciting and well-crafted ... Rivard's short short stories are carefully written narratives that provide glimpses into the lives of some very unusual people ... poignant ... heartbreaking and honest…the best capture the telling moments of life with humour and compassion … engaging."

— Debbie Howlett, *Quill & Quire*

FRANKIE'S DESIRES
(POETRY, 1987)

"Rivard feels closer to the down and out than to the high and mighty. Frankie, whose frank desires, devilish sense of humour and ironic awareness of his own devilishness, makes the book lively. Rivard is a fine reporter of the foibles of this protagonist. The wit is rich and typical of the tone of this artfully sophisticated but innocent even simple looking work. Like Frost before him, Rivard is touching the heart with Frankie's apparent naivete, only pretending to be Everyman. This lovely, lively, loving work will be the most important repositioning of a Canadian poet to appear this year…establishes him (Rivard) as a powerful writer and this collection is recommended for libraries with Commonwealth, Canadian and contemporary shelves. Rivard, the Calgary poet of the unforgettable Frankie will be heard from again and again."

— Robert Solomon, *Small Press*

"Frankie ain't beautiful but he's audaciously real."

— Mark Lowey, *Calgary Herald*

"Ken Rivard's poems are sad/funny reflections of ourselves as we dream-desire our way through the maze that is defined as life. His verse lines echo in the ears of all who would listen to him."

– Michael O'Nowlan, *Canadian Book Review Annual*

"*Frankie's Desires* becomes ours — to live — to open up to — to understand."

— Gerald Hill, *Edmonton Journal*

KISS ME DOWN TO SIZE
(POETRY, 1983)

"Sense of commitment…written from the engaged stance of an observing human being in this world. Rivard keeps a trained eye (and ear) on the emotional energy that lies in wait beneath the lines. It is not written by a pompous poet in capital letters. Its voice is gentle, insistent in its quiet way and everywhere fraught with a concurrent sense of humility and necessity."

— Judith Fitzgerald, *Canadian Literature*

"Rivard has a good sense of when to spin out and where it should go. And he nicely flips a surreal attachment to many of his statements."

— Michael Cullen, *Out of the Blue*

"Presents with bracing force a regional voice that is astringent almost impossible to ignore."

— Allan Hustak, *Alberta Report*

"Writes in simple, colloquial diction … uses spare language, an unadorned style."

— Anne Burke, *Writers' Quarterly*

"Rivard's essential humanism is obvious … [He] is able to write emphatically about elderly and young alike … diction and imagery are strong and pleasing."

— Martin Singleton, *Canadian Book Review Annual*

"The most impressive aspect of Rivard's work is its tendency towards a surrealistic, dream-like quality."

— Bob Attridge, *Newest Annual*

UP FRONT

UP FRONT

FLASH FICTION

Ken Rivard

Library and Archives Canada Cataloguing in Publication

Title: Up front: flash fiction / Ken Rivard.

Other titles: Canal watch

Names: Rivard, Ken, 1947- author.

Identifiers: Canadiana (print) 20240338987 |
               Canadiana (ebook) 20240338995 |

ISBN 9781771617604 (softcover) | ISBN 9781771617611 (PDF) |
ISBN 9781771617628 (EPUB) | ISBN 9781771617635 (Kindle)

Subjects: LCGFT: Flash fiction.
Classification: LCC PS8585.I8763 U62 2024 | DDC C813/.54—dc23

Published by Mosaic Press, Oakville, Ontario, Canada, 2024.
MOSAIC PRESS, Publishers
www.Mosaic-Press.com
Copyright © Ken Rivard, 2024

Printed and bound in Canada.

ONTARIO ARTS COUNCIL
CONSEIL DES ARTS DE L'ONTARIO
an Ontario government agency
un organisme du gouvernement de l'Ontario

Funded by the Government of Canada
Financé par le gouvernement du Canada

ONTARIO CREATES

MOSAIC PRESS
1252 Speers Road, Units 1 & 2, Oakville, Ontario, L6L 2X4
(905) 825-2130 • info@mosaic-press.com • www.mosaic-press.com

OTHER BOOKS BY KEN RIVARD

FICTION

CanalWatch (flash fiction, Mosaic Press, 2022)

Motherwild (novel, Thistledown Press, 2014)

Missionary Positions (postcard/flash fiction, Black Moss Press, 2008)

Whiskey Eyes (postcard/flash fiction, Black Moss Press, 2004)

Bottle Talk (postcard/flash fiction, Black Moss Press, 2002)

Skin Tests (postcard/flash fiction, Black Moss Press, 2000)

If She Could Take All These Men (postcard/flash fiction/ prose poetry, Beach Holme Publishing, 1995)

POETRY

Frankie's Desires (Quarry Press, 1987).

Kiss Me Down to Size (Thistledown Press, 1983)

CHILDREN'S LITERATURE

The Trouble with Uncle Kevin (Calgary Communities Against Sexual Abuse, 2007, 2023)

Mom, the School Flooded (Annick Press, 1996, 2007)

ACKNOWLEDGMENTS AND AUTHOR'S NOTES

THIS BOOK IS FOR H.P. AND A PAST LIFE. A MUCH EARLIER version/draft was originally accepted as part of the requirements for a Master's Degree program from McGill University. Special thanks to Micheline, Annie and Melissa for who they are and for their continued belief in my writing.

A portion of UP FRONT appeared in PRAIRIE JOURNAL OF CANADIAN LITERATURE.

These stories do not in any way claim to be the truth. Nonetheless, they are inspired by actual events. UP FRONT is a "what if?" book. It is a series of flash fiction stories, each approximately 500 words (and one even longer) in length, and are based on events during the beginning years (12-13 years olds) and the ending years (17–18 years olds) in an inner-city, secondary school. Each story asks "what if? and attempts to capture the energy of a specific moment in the real lives of adolescents. Occasionally a story turns back on itself with the first line becoming the last line, resulting in a kind of framed story moment. Not every flash fiction piece progressively builds more tension or moves towards a new understanding, or even closure because many of life's moments are ongoing. Open-ended stories allow readers to create their own conclusions. From time to time, readers may also be asked to suspend their disbelief. Enjoy!

"Memory is almost always fragmentized, sanitized, demonized or wholly fictionalized by its constant travel companion and fickle lover, imagination."

— Stephen Mack Jones

"One great use of words is to hide our thoughts."

— Voltaire

CONTENTS

FIRST DAYS

LAST DAYS

FIRST DAYS

Tinge

As soon as the girl opens her book, a droplet of joy trickles down the girl's forehead, curls between different-sized freckles on her small, hawkish nose and rolls onto her top lip. Then her mouth relaxes with one lip barely touching the other and her smile is so light it could float across the room and out a window or under the door. On her own island, or ocean, or mountain-top, the girl's right hand strokes the page of her book and the width of her grin opens her face to the world. A right leg crosses a left leg and the tips of her red and blue runners lean against each other, like best friends. Her eyes, the colour of dates, look uneasy, as if they are checking for a sudden noise or boiling water on a stove. Wearing what looks like new black jeans, she is perhaps delaying the removal of the store label until the jeans feel just right. Hanging from her shoulders, a shocking-pink sweater clings to her torso and might be an enormous pink petal of a mysterious tropical flower.

Perhaps at her age of twelve, the girl notices that others in the room are not as in love with print as she is; she inhales stories while others simply inhale. Several months ago, the girl wrote to an author telling him that his stories were meant only for her and, of course, the author wholeheartedly agreed in his written reply. Could she be gradually finding herself on every page because her face is its own narrative?

3

Lifting her eyes, the girl watches several boys and girls checking their cellphones and texting under their desks. A boy in the far corner of the room has an earphone hidden under his longish chestnut hair, but his closed eyes and swaying head give him away.

Maybe the girl's parents currently refuse to buy her a cellphone or any other electronic device because they refuse to have her isolated from the reality of in-person dialogue.

Meanwhile the print in her book has swallowed her whole. Words flow just below the surface of the girl's skin... on her face, neck, arms and probably body too, like fish swimming around pebbles in a stream. She is now a living, breathing character in her story and wears her make believe like some people wear a comfortable sweater. And the girl pushes back her blonde hair, as if the hair is a blank page belonging to her book.

The voice up front strolls by her desk and nods for a split second. Why interrupt her? Now that the girl's eyes are glazed over, nothing the voice up front says or does will make a difference. Besides, her elation takes direction from no one because joy has its own legs.

"I wish I were her," the voice up front whispers to itself.

"I am her," says the girl to herself, as if she heard the murmur clearly.

Then the boy with the earphones is told by the voice up front to unplug his device.

As she sighs deeply, the girl gently closes her book to the day outside her story.

Later, when she arrives home, she may be ready to remove the store label from her black jeans and then turn another page.

Will she be in her next story?

Recipe

RED IS THE COLOUR OF HIS RECIPE.

What is going on? More and more hands stop keyboarding. Fingers become ears.

A boy over by the wall does not care because no one would believe the story he writes. He looks down at the backs of his hands and sees one red scar on his right hand and two on the other, each about the size of an eraser on the end of a pencil. As his fingers peck at the keyboard, the scars dance up and down and back and forth like blood-dried little characters.

"Does your story hurt you?" asks the voice up front.

And the boy looks first at the voice up front and then his fingers, but says nothing.

Several days ago, two of the boy's much older cousins stormed into his house late at night, the smell of beer and vomit all over them. Quickly the two men stumbled into the boy's bedroom. One man sat on the boy's chest and pinned his arms to the bed while the other used a lit cigarette and burned three holes on the backs of the boy's hands. The harder the boy kicked and screamed, the more the two men laughed. The boy cried louder and louder until he lost his voice to the grip of torture. Then the two cousins mimicked their voice-less cousin some more, as if there was no difference between laughter and pain. After they set the boy free, he ran into the bathroom and turned on the cold water tap for relief. Finally, the cousins staggered out of the house opening and closing their mouths in a continuous pantomime of mockery.

Meanwhile the boy's parents are out playing Bingo and having a few cold ones. And when they return, their son is still voiceless as he drowns his hands in the bathroom sink filled with water and now ice cubes.

"You'll be alright," the mother slurs.

"Yeah, you'll be fine after a good night's sleep," the father mumbles.

The next morning, after the boy goes to see the school nurse, he returns to the room with bandages on the backs of his hands.

"Do you have to read our writing aloud afterwards?" he asks the voice up front.

"No," the voice up front replies. "Why do you ask?"

"It's our own silent recipe. My family does its own preparing, if you know what I mean, so we cook up our own stories too. After all, it is not all like Valentine's Day out there. I never get any hearts and flowers from anyone. Got it?"

"Yes, I certainly do," replies the voice up front. "Follow your own directions."

Today the boy will continue his endless story which will not be shared.

Red is the colour of his recipe.

Good Morning

HE DOES IT ALL WITHOUT WATERING UP HIS EYES.

Zigzagging down the corridor, the boy slams shut two lockers and brushes a girl in her bloused rib cage. As he elbows still another girl in her purse, the boy slows down his bulldozing and says, "Good Morning, Good Morning, Good Morning," to no one in particular.

The boy, wearing a striped green and blue T-shirt, orange runners and faded blue jeans, slides into his chair and plants his elbows on top of his thighs. His light brown hair is combed back so perfectly, he looks as if he is prepared to say "Good Morning" to a TV camera and then do a commercial about a breakfast cereal.

However, inside he is not done yet. His grandfather died a few days ago and the boy's pain still simmers. The grandfather's last words to him were: "Good Morning." At the time, the voice up front was also notified of the grandfather's passing by the boy's mother.

Before he left home this morning, the boy's mother said it was time to start over again and that he had to shut down his tears. He learned his part. The boy practiced standing in front of the bathroom mirror with his mother beside him. He rehearsed saying, "Good Morning" without watering up his eyes. He tried and tried so hard that his face nearly exploded. Then his grief found another way to leave when

7

his mother taught her son how to push his tears backwards and swallow them.

Now in the room with his arms planted on his desk and holding up his head, the boy reminds his friend sitting beside him that, as of this morning, he will start all over again.

"How do you do that?" his much taller friend asks. "Don't you have to die first, like your grandfather?"

"Do I look like I want to die?"

"No."

"Then what are you trying to tell me?"

"It's your grandpa. It's like he's sitting right there beside you!"

"So?"

"You must have said 'Good Morning' at least ten times when you burst in today."

The Good Morning boy removes his hands from his face. Then he raises his right arm toward the ceiling.

"Need to go to the washroom," he announces to the voice up front.

"But you just got here," the voice up front replies.

"I know, I know, but I really have to go!" the boy answers, swallowing as fast as he can.

"Go ahead."

Down the hallway, a bathroom door slams and a squeaky tap is turned on and off, as if it were a performance of sorts.

Lipstick

SHE LIVES TO VIBRATE.

The short, plump, blue-eyed girl, dressed in rose-coloured pants and blouse, quivers and shakes when she enters the room, as if her body has disappeared beneath her excess weight. Her iPod's going full blast. In her huge purse, which is a mound of green suede, she searches frantically for something. At her desk, the purse opens to a bowlful of October fields. Pens and combs battle each other. Orange and white tissues explode into a flurry of Halloween. Keys rattle. A wallet thumps onto the floor. A purple comb appears. A smaller orange comb follows. She digs and digs as pieces from her life flutter into the air. Then she stops after finding her cellphone under three packs of opened spearmint chewing gum.

Picking up her cellphone, the girl calls home and asks someone that burning question: "Where is it?"

"How am I supposed to know?" a voice at the other end says.

"But you always know where everything is!" the girl insists.

"Hey, it's your purse, not mine!" the voice at the other end says.

"Please check on my dresser or in the bathroom."

There is a long pause as the girl moves her cellphone from one ear to another and the fingers on her free hand tap, tap, tap on her desk.

"I have looked everywhere. Besides, what am I... your maid?"

"Try the living room and kitchen, will you? Please!"

"Okay, okay. Hang on!"

Moments later the voice at the other end returns and says: "No luck."

"I can't talk without it," the girl says into her cellphone. "I can hardly breathe either."

"What do you think you're doing now?" asks the voice at the other end.

"I'm not going to make it without my lipstick!"

"Come on. Look harder," the other voice answers.

Then the girl pours the rest of the contents onto her desk until the pile becomes a heap of items from one of those shopping mall vending machines. Slowly, she picks her way through everything on her desk and next to the corrugated shirtsleeves of a hunchback apple tree, she finds her... lipstick.

"Got it," she yells into her cellphone. "Hello. Hello!"

A voice on the intercom blurts out the singing of the national anthem, the song coming from a long, hollow tube and the day begins.

Planning

"COULD BE," THE GIRL AT THE BACK ANNOUNCES OVER HER shoulder, her voice as smooth as beach pebbles.

In the locker room behind the classroom, six girls slap on makeup, as if doing it for the first time and their cheeks become a source of curiosity.

One girl uses a dusty window as a mirror and she instantly becomes the woman she always wanted to be. Dragging whispered strategies from one side of the window to the other, she becomes a pocket-sized adult figuring out her day. Then she stands ready and waiting for the other girls to line up behind her. One by one, the line behind her forms in silence and occasional giggling with each girl asking the one behind how she looks.

"Looks cool to me," the lead girl says to the one behind her.

"Not bad," another girl says.

"Sexy," a third girl adds while laughing red-faced.

And the same words become dominoes moving down the line until almost everyone appears ready.

"But I feel like a clown and I stink like one too," the girl at the end of the line says. "Why am I wearing this crap, anyway?"

"You know why," the lead girl announces. "And clowns do not stink!"

"For sure," says the second girl.

"Of course," replies the third.

"Why do you even wonder?" the fourth girl asks.

"You know better than that," adds the fifth girl.

"Yes, I do know better," the last girl replies. And she rubs and rubs her face so hard that her reddened skin is ready to burst from her face.

Mirrors click open. Faces get checked. The morning sun screams through the only window. Lockers creak open and then slam shut. The voice up front approaches the locker room. A chorus of shushing bounces off the walls. Faces aim straight ahead. The procession of girls gets ready.

"Now, you really all look like circus clowns in a horror movie," the last girl proclaims to a row of laughter.

"You are the real clowns. Not me. Screw you!"

"Now, now, be nice so we can all get ready to start the day," says the lead girl straightening her shoulders.

"Yes," says the second girl.

"Of course," the third girl replies throwing her head back, her long hair moving like waves.

"Let's stop wondering about it," the fourth girl says raising her voice. "And just go!"

"We know better," the fifth girl says. "And... we also know a real clown when we see one."

"Are you girls ready?" asks the voice up front sticking its nose into the locker room.

"Does anyone here look kind of funny to you?" the first girl asks the voice up front.

"Nope, but I sure can smell the make-up. Are you girls planning something today?"

Pausing, the girls breathe in who they are and proceed out of the locker room and into the day.

"Could be," the girl at the back announces over her shoulder, her voice again inventing calmness.

Red

BLOOD HAS A MIND OF ITS OWN.

Midway down the row by the window, a dandelion girl develops a facial alphabet of her own... her face bent, twisted and buckled under her pain. The girl's face has its own vocabulary. She only found out this morning for the first time from her mother, who was in no hurry... to inform about blood.

The voice up front notices the girl's severe discomfort.

"Can I see you outside for a moment?" the voice up front asks.

"I guess so," replies the girl as she follows the voice out of the room.

In the hallway, they both speak in whispers, as if the hallway lockers had ears.

"It's all over your face. You look like you're not feeling well."

"I'm not," the girl replies.

"Anything I can do to help?

"Nope."

"But you are obviously hurting."

"So?"

"Is your stomach upset? Do you have the flu?"

"Nah, I don't feel like puking."

"Is there something else like maybe a bad headache?"

"No, but it's my first one."

"First what?" asked the voice up front.

"First...you know what happens to girls once a month."

"Oh, sure. I have two daughters at home."

"Ah, I may as well tell you. Before I left for school, my big brother asked me if I was on the pad or the rag and I was not sure what he meant."

"So maybe you should go see the school nurse and have a talk with her? I can walk you down there if you want," suggests the voice up front.

"What can the nurse do?"

"Maybe... she can help you with that pain. Give her a try."

"Listen, my mother waited until this morning to tell me about all this because she said no one can help me with my cramps. What is that supposed to mean?"

"I do not know. Some mothers may be afraid or do not know how to tell. Some mothers know how to tell but do not want to. Not sure."

"So...how does that help make it all go away?"

"Good question."

"Also, why can't the blood just go back to where it came from?" she asks.

Blood has a mind of its own.

Clocks

THE CLOCK IS LOUDER THAN EVER.

Clusters of kids almost squish into each other and anxiously wait in the doorway for the lunch bell to ring, but nothing happens.

Words from the intercom tell all students to go back to their desks and the voice up front is to lock the room door.

A minute later, another intercom voice says that the building is in a lockdown and that everyone is to take cover under desks. The voice up front also ducks behind its desk. Room lights are turned off. Under their desks, boys and girls are too scared to talk or move or even try to eat. Only measured breathing and the ticking sounds of the silver wall clock over the doorway can be heard.

Suddenly there is a loud banging on the narrow window of the door. A man in dark blue suit, white shirt and red-striped tie has his nose squished up against the window and shouts. "Let me in! I know my daughter is in there. I want to see her right away. She belongs to me! Only me! Do you hear me? Let me in. I can see some of you under your desks so let me in!"

No one moves. The clock ticks louder...louder.

Eventually, the man at the door removes his smudged, oily face from the window and leaves, his voice muttering something as it trails down the hallway...marbles clattering.

Moments after that, an announcement on the intercom says that all is clear and that the building is safe. The voice up front emerges from under its desk and asks if everyone is okay. Lights are turned on. Bodies slide out from under desks. Everyone, except for one girl, is ready at the door with lunches stuffed under arms.

The voice up front moves cautiously over to the girl's desk and says: "Okay. You can come out now."

"No, no, my father's still out there…somewhere," says the girl. "I know what he's like!"

"Believe me, if the principal says it's safe, it's safe. Come on out."

"Can you come home with me tonight?" the girl pleads with the voice up front whose tongue is immediately tied.

"And maybe, the principal can come too?"

The voice up front unlocks the door, looks both ways outside and then carefully pushes the door open.

Boys and girls move noiselessly into the hallway and head towards the gym, as if silence is the only source of survival. When they get to the gym, they scatter to their favourite spots on the floor and leaving behind only a trail of quiet, like crumbs from their sandwiches. Food is stuffed into mouths. Only tremors of gulping slacken their consumption.

Meanwhile back in the room, with the door wide open, the voice up front eats its own lunch with the girl eating hers sitting nearby. Crusts lay by their elbows right next to their hope and the clock barely ticks.

Last One

He is the last one to hand it in.

The redheaded boy is as tall as the caretaker's broom handle and almost as thin. His chest bone protrudes from above his purple T-shirt, as if he too had been hung out to dry with yesterday's laundry. The boy's nose could belong to another mammal and his forehead is forever pinched into a frown. Clusters of freckles on his knuckles are mostly box-brown in colour. His shoulders are turned inward, as if they are brackets holding him together. With eyes the colour of a blue Holiday Inn roof, this boy focusses so hard on getting ready for the exam that the Holiday Inn roof outside could be blown off and no one would notice.

But another male student across from him notices something when the redheaded boy stands up. Yes, he notices that the kid's zipper is completely down. Should he tell him? Should he point down there and nod? The redheaded boy does not notice the looks from the other student as everyone stands and moves on to the next class.

In the hallway, other fingers and eyes point at the red-headed boy. His determined concentration does not waver. Exam anticipation fills the boy's mind, like the mud on a road after a flood. When students stroll into their next class, a few snickers are aimed at the boy with the fallen zipper.

"Can I have a word with you, outside?" the voice up front asks casually.

Out in the hallway, while pointing at its own zipper, the voice's low tone tells the boy about flying half-mast. He quickly zips up and follows the voice up front back into the room.

At his desk, the boy meets every smile coming his way with an easy grin of his own.

"Okay everyone, start writing and good luck," the voice up front announces.

Papers crinkle. Eyes focus. Feet shuffle. Chairs creak. And the faint sounds of pencil or pen on paper fill the air. The voice up front moves up and down the rows to make sure all is well. When he reaches the redheaded boy, the voice up front stops, gives him a half-smile and then moves on.

Then the boy quickly looks down at his zipper and back again at the exam. His zipper is partially down. Again.

"Must have something to do with these new jeans or the way I'm sitting or...," the boy mutters, as he pulls up his fly once again. His powers of retention might depend on the tiny gold teeth of his zipper.

Perhaps while writing the exam, the boy sometimes sees himself as a cartoon character struggling up a gigantic zipper as he tries to find the right answers. And maybe other times he rehearses walking out of the room and carrying a mystery novel just below his belt to cover any evidence.

Gunpowder

She hears that only boys blow up trees.

Off they go to the lab to try their hands at Bunsen burners for the first time. The eyes of a long-legged, black-haired girl with the permanent tan seem to be preoccupied with something beyond the world of science.

On the weekend, the same girl got her hands on some of her father's gunpowder. She and her best friend used a straw and poured the explosive into the holes of a small tree in the park. Then the girls blew up the tree when they thought no one was around. To see the bark and wood flying everywhere, like confetti, the bleeding wood, pieces of leaves scattered… their faces ripped, was a huge thrill for both girls. Scary blast! Exciting noise! The two girls figured they would never get caught. Besides, gunpowder has no gender.

Now in the lab, boys and girls are shown how to light their Bunsen burners. Both girls hunch over and watch the blue flame thump and whoosh to life. Everyone else in class looks back and forth from the voice up front to the Bunsen burner and waits for further directions. Fixated on the flame, the two friends may be reliving the tree explosion.

The long-legged girl still has some of her father's gunpowder left in a pill container in her jean pocket. She considers dropping a little powder on her flame and the imagined thrill of it all. The girl may see her Bunsen burner blowing both her and her best friend's faces everywhere, their noses, cheeks, lips… skin sticking to the voice up front's white lab coat. She hears her classmates screaming and yelling and scattering. She hears the fire alarm, the sirens. She imagines the voice up front walking like a zombie out into the hallway and then downstairs to the staffroom. There, the voice asks everyone why an adolescent would do such a thing. Is it because of fascination or puberty stumbling over itself?

"I need a washroom break," she says to the voice up front.

"Sure," answers the voice. "Your Bunsen burner will be waiting for you."

"Thanks," the long-legged girl says getting up from her stool.

Outside in the hallway, the girl drags her feet on the freshly polished floor on her way to the washroom, her fingers gripping the pill container in her jeans. In the washroom, she peers into the mirror, pauses, pictures face pieces plastered on the looking glass and then shakes her gunpowder visions into the sink, like salt.

She hears that only boys blow up trees.

Easier to Tell

My breathing almost stops.

"I did not budge. I stayed in bed afraid to wet my pants, but I did anyway, as if my body were being emptied of pee," the boy with short black hair and blue eyes says to his friend in the yard.

"Why didn't you get up before you had that first wet spot?" the friend asks.

"Ma said I had to stay in bed until everyone got up, no matter what. Pa insisted on it too."

"Why?"

"A few years back I got up very early and went for a bike ride. My parents got scared when they noticed I was gone."

"Yeah, but forcing you to stay in bed is crazy. You are now twelve years old. Most people do not pee in bed at the age of twelve... or do they?"

"I know. I know. Everyone in class is tired of me asking to go to the washroom. The other day the voice up front asked me if I could wait a bit. I held it in as long as possible but when I stood up, I... I suddenly felt that warm wet spot on my jeans."

"Isn't... isn't there a name for that?" asks the friend.

"Not sure," says the boy.

"By the way, what did you think when the voice told us his first name and we all said "'just like the hockey goalie."'

"What does that have to do with the dark pee stain on my jeans?"

"There's a name for everything."

"What do hockey goalies do if they have to have a pee?"

"Ask the voice up front. The voice likes hockey," the friend says.

"But there's no way I'm going to tell the voice about my wet spot," insists the boy.

"Make up a story. Pretend you are talking about someone you know."

"But my jeans don't pretend."

"Something makes you pee at the wrong times. Find out! What do your parents say about it?

"They're afraid and if it happens again today, they'll take me to the doctor."

"So what are they waiting for?" the friend asks.

"Maybe for my pee story to end," answers the boy.

"Why?"

"I really do not know. Maybe the story's easier to tell when it is over."

The Banana Boat Wait

WILL THE BANANA BOAT WAIT BRING CLARITY TO THEIR LIVES? Will it?

With their heads bowed in submission, each looks at one another, as if wanting to blurt out anything into the eerie quiet. The goose bumps around their pores spell the word "fear" on their arms. All three of them have committed something that has crossed all boundaries but what... did they do?

The tallest boy, crouched forward into himself, like a question mark, scratches the sides of his head with his fingernails of both hands. Excuses run rampant under his itchy scalp. His light brown hair is so long on top and so short on the sides, he could use the top of his head to mop the floor. He can be heard mumbling to himself, rehearsing his lies. Then the boy chews on a fingernail and grinds it all into tasty dust, the outline of which can be seen ebbing down his throat. His right leg crosses over his left leg and then he reverses the process over and over until the quickness of his breath brings his legs to rest.

The second boy is almost the same height as the first boy but weighs about thirty pounds more. His lips are scrunched together, like uneven flames, as if his mouth is on fire. His designer jeans are too big for him...possible hand-me-downs from an older brother. The noises coming from his stomach are loud and it is difficult to know if the sounds are from hunger or from just being here today. He picks at his left shirtsleeve and looks at the floor moving his eyes back and forth, as if scanning the floor tiles for comfort.

Short and wiry the third boy looks almost ready for whatever happens. His confidence might be building because he now stares straight ahead, shrugs his shoulders at the other boys and then flings his hands, palms up, to the light above. His legs and feet remain still for the most part and his elbows now rest easily on the arms of his chair. Soon however, the boy's purple shirt has dark blotches growing from the armpits that might be lost continents adrift in an unnamed ocean just as the burgundy sun sets. And the big toe in his left shoe moves up and down ready to explode from the leather.

Suddenly the Principal appears and says: "You, you and you… in my office."

All three boys stand and march away from their waiting.

The bell rings and the Principal says: "You boys aren't going anywhere-now or ever."

"What is going to happen to us?" the shortest boy asks, his voice sounding flat in the late afternoon sunlight streaming in from the window. The boy's forehead sweats its own alphabet, as if his forehead is the real indicator of who he is behind his Clint Eastwood façade.

"Wouldn't you like to know? However, before I start, the three of you should just plan to get jobs on a banana boat. Yes, loading and unloading bananas. Nothing more. I am not usually this harsh but a banana boat job is about the best you will ever accomplish. But first I will have the Secretary call your parents and tell them you will be late."

"But I have a dentist appointment," the first boy says.

"I have to get supper ready," blurts out the second boy.

"And I better get home to pack for that banana boat," says the third boy.

"Wise guy, eh? Forget the dentist and supper!" the Principal mutters.

"What about that banana boat job?" the third boy asks.

"Easy. It will always be waiting. For all of you," announces the Principal, his right hand sweeping across the incoming sunlight and dismissing their cringing faces.

Will the banana boat wait bring clarity to their lives? Will it?

Lip Reading

THE BOY SHOULD HAVE BEEN BORN ON THE OTHER SIDE OF THE glass.

The voice up front watches everyone working in groups and moves its way elsewhere between two boys talking in a corner of the room.

"My dad left town. I think he went to Halifax."

"What happened?"

"He just got out of jail and squealed on two guys who helped him try to rob a bank."

"And?"

"And the two guys are now in jail, but they have friends on the outside," says the first boy.

"So, your dad's scared that the friends might go after him? Sounds like a TV show," answers the second boy.

"It is not TV. He KNOWS they will be coming after him."

"What about your mom? She must be worried!"

"My dad told her not to try and contact him. He will find a way to get in touch with her somehow."

"That's scary stuff."

"Yeah, my two brothers and sister were crying this morning," the boy says turning his eyes away.

"You look tired, beat," the voice up front says.

"I had a crappy sleep. I know we all have dreams but... I dreamed that I would not see my dad for many years and forgot how he looked. In my sleep I was a man and I travelled to Halifax by myself to see him and found out he was in jail again. I tried everything to get him out. I even threw a rope over the prison wall but the rope was never long enough!" the first boy says.

"Weird dream. Were you able to talk to your dad at all?" asks the second boy.

"Just for a short time during a visit, but he was behind a glass wall and we talked on a phone that didn't work that well and... ."

"What did you talk about?"

"Like I said, I could not hear him that well, but he could hear me, I thought, so I did most of the talking and I wondered if he still cared about me. I had to know so I watched his face to see where his talking was coming from."

"What did you see?" the second boy asks.

The voice up front's ears become all ears.

Then, another boy nearby asks out of nowhere: "I need your help."

"I'll be right there" the voice up front says.

"But... ."

"Wait your turn."

"Awwww," the other boy says.

"So, did you find out if your father cared about you?" asks the voice up front now standing nearby.

"Nope, I could only read my father's lips at the start but after that I couldn't be sure if he cared about me or not," he tells the voice up front. "And something I learned the last few years... just because someone is looking you in the eye doesn't mean he or she is telling the truth."

The boy should have been born on the other side of the glass.

Locks

THE BLONDE, FRIZZY-HAIRED GIRL WITH THE LARGE MAGNET really wants to know about my keys.

With hair as black as midnight, the other girl is almost as tall as the length of her ponytail which hangs down behind almost to the backs of her knees, like an exclamation mark. Her face is tight and the start of a crow's foot is faintly carved on the outside of each of her huge blue eyes. Something lumpy might be continually swimming back and forth inside her chest.

"Every night, Daddy bolts us inside our apartment to keep outsiders outside," the dark-haired girl tells the voice up front.

"Why is that?" asks the voice up front.

"Well, even my nearly blind grandpa helps Daddy lock us in at night. We have six locks on our front door. When any part of the moon is showing, which is almost all the time, both Daddy and Grandpa sit close to each other and whisper scary stories to each other, stories that they never share with us," she says, her eyes becoming bright blue moons as she pulls her knees closer together.

"Between stories, one of them gets up and checks to make sure the front door is safe. Each lock is unlocked and locked again. The seventh lock heard is when Daddy unlocks the drawer where he keeps his loaded pistol."

28

Almost immediately she points the index finger of her right hand towards the voice up front.

"At first my mom just smiled and assumed that they were taking care of our safety. Then last week, Daddy mentioned at supper that he was also thinking of putting locks on each of our bedroom doors. Mom reminded him that this would only keep us locked up even more and what would we do if a key got lost."

The girl then flings her hands towards the walls, as if each finger had tried looking for answers.

"Daddy always has a plan. Whenever we leave the apartment, we need to wear copies of all the keys around our necks. But only Daddy has the key to the gun drawer. We remember which key is which because each has a number taped to the top. Number One key is for the top lock on the front door. Number Two key is for the second lock from the top and so on all the way down to lock Number Six." And the girl re-counts each key on her fingers making sure the voice up front counts along with her.

"The other day my friend with the huge magnet stood close to me and made all my keys push out from under my blouse. It looked like I had eight little, weird boobies growing all over my chest instead of two. I was shocked into laughing and crying at the same time. The girl with the magnet really wanted to know about each key... especially this one," she said holding up the largest key. "She really had to know why I had so many around my neck so I told her the keys protect me. Does your magnet protect you? "I asked her.

The girl wanted me to prove it so I told her to come for a sleepover this coming Friday night and to bring her magnet. She will find out about all my keys."

Because of Fingers

It had to be a finger trick.

"I couldn't do my work last night."

The Latino boy is too tall for his skin and his puberty makes him look like a broomstick. His knees almost bang together and could belong to two different boys. On his chin, a pimple is a beacon demanding immediate attention.

"Can I talk to you?" he asks.

"Sure," answers the voice up front.

"Couldn't get my work done."

"And?"

"My parents were fighting all night."

"Again?"

"Of course."

"What happened?"

"It's my father. My mother says he spends too much money," the boy says.

"How does he do that?"

"Once a week he disappears and comes home with empty pockets."

"Do you know where he goes?"

"We finally found out last night that he is taking private magic lessons. That made me curious and I put away my work so I could listen outside my parents' bedroom door."

"So, what did you find out?" the voice up front asks.

"He said that this woman magician was showing him all the tricks that women love."

"And?"

"And my mother asked him to try out one of the woman's tricks on her."

"What happened?"

"Well, my father held up his two hands with his fingers spread out like two fans. He told my mother to pick a finger and he would make that finger disappear and then find it later."

"What did he mean by that?"

"I am not sure, but my mother got so mad, she said she would cut off more than his finger if he had been fooling around with that woman magician. Well, that made him madder than mad," the boy says.

"Was it more than disappearing fingers," the voice up front adds creating a question mark of skin on its forehead.

"Does it matter what it is?"

"Probably."

"In my house, my dog has more brains than my father," the boy replies patting an invisible animal by his knee.

"Really now. How can you tell?" the voice up front asks sitting up straighter in its desk.

"My dog has timing. She knows when to do her tricks and my father... he will never learn."

"Well, at least your dog has learned and done its own homework."

"Very funny. I lied. I do not have a dog," the boy says. "But I do have a... father."

Subway Boys

As if the sun suddenly dropped from the sky, the voice up front loses itself after hearing what happened.

At the end of the day, war whoops, laughing, scampering, and shouting suddenly all become blurts and new noises as one by one, bodies stuff through the turnstiles. On the other side, they wait for one another and then let the escalator bring them down to the platform. All are supposed to stand behind the yellow line until the subway cars arrive, come to a full stop and the doors whoosh open.

However, two boys dance back and forth across the yellow line. The first boy has dark brown hair and is much taller than his friend whose hair is an explosion of night. The skin on his face is a perfect cloud white. The second boy is a head shorter and dressed in denim, has pasty skin craving sun. Both boys need dancing lessons of any kind.

The boys taunt the tracks below, as if the lines of steel dare them to do something. Then the sound of a coming subway can be heard from the tunnel to the left.

A man's voice yells out: "Get back behind that yellow line or you'll get hurt or maybe killed!"

"No way, I'll never die." the dark-haired boy shouts back.

The dark-haired boy remembers a story that the voice up front had read earlier that day. And believe it or not, the story is about a man whose final wish was to dance on his own grave.

32

As the sound of the oncoming train gets louder, the boys increase the speed of their dance, zipping back and forth across the yellow line. The two daredevils wave towards the tunnel, as if ready for any challenge. Just as the spotlight on the first car becomes a glare, one of the boys sticks out his arm, fingers stretched to see if he can touch the passing blue cars. However, the tall, white-faced boy suddenly loses his bravado and jumps back.

As the subway cars zoom by, there is a muffled scream and bloody fingers float through the air... fleshy digits going nowhere. People wince and duck at the same time. A few wipe away drops of blood from their faces and clothing. Several onlookers rush over to the boy now rolling back and forth on the yellow line and screaming the skin off his face. His friend keeps pacing back and forth and yells for help. Others stand stunned and several drop their backpacks and bags.

The subways cars screech to a stop so suddenly passengers inside are thrown to the floor. Doors open. People crawl out. The driver calls for help. One woman carrying a Hudson's Bay shopping bag, removes her jacket, rolls it up and slips it under the injured boy's head. Quickly removing his own beige sweater, a man wraps it around the boy's bleeding, fingerless hand. Then the dark-haired boy faints, his head limp by his right shoulder, a dropped bag of fruit.

"Let us through! Let us through," a paramedic yells.

"Please stop the bleeding," someone shouts.

Before long the boy is strapped to a stretcher and then carried quickly up the escalator. The man who tried to warn the boys follows closely behind. Commuters on the moving steel steps quickly squeeze to the right to make room. The man following the stretcher gasps and mutters all the way to the exit... something about never warning anyone again and his words burst through the doorway into the late afternoon sky, like lost subway dust.

As if the sun suddenly dropped from the sky, the voice up front loses itself after hearing what happened.

Eye

BECAUSE HER RIGHT EYE IS MADE OF GLASS, THE GIRL'S LEFT EYE simmers with passion.

At the doorway to the room, the girl with the orange hair stands in her faded blue jeans and bright red blouse almost lecturing to a male friend and gesturing at the walls and ceiling, as if someone's life were on the line. The girl's message becomes so urgent that her male friend's T-shirt seems to be fading from pale green to white the more she emphasizes each of her words. Stepping backwards until his shoulders touch the wall and his own eyes are as wide as the fire alarm device attached to the wall near his head, the boy develops new ways of cowering.

"Whatever happens, don't tell anyone about my glass eye!" she says, her finger stabbing the boy's chest. "I want to be treated like everyone else!"

"I promise, I won't," he answers, slowly curling the girl's finger towards the floor with his right hand. "Your eye will be a secret but... what makes you think that the voice up front won't treat you like everyone else?"

Soon the bell rings and everyone files into the room. The girl prepares for the discussion about yesterday's story students were asked to read, a story about a man who misplaces his wooden leg, even though we are told that artificial legs are no longer made of wood. Of course, he blames his friend. Both he and his friend had too much to drink the evening before and the man with the wooden leg got into one of his rants about injustice. The friend had finally told him that if he did not shut up, he would use his friend's wooden leg for firewood. This enraged the man with the wooden leg and he lectured even louder to his friend on the social inequalities faced by handicapped people. Then both friends fell asleep across from one another, one on the sofa and the other in a rocking chair.

When he awoke the next morning, the man's wooden leg was gone, but there was still wood smouldering in the fireplace.

And the opening question from the voice up front was: "Do you think that the man actually burnt his friend's wooden leg?"

"Yes," the girl with the glass eye blurts out before anyone else has a chance to speak.

"Really?" the voice up front asks. "How do you know?"

"Well, it is obvious, isn't it? This story is a bad joke. And I hate it!"

"Look around. Nobody's laughing. And you do not have to like the story either. What if the man woke up before his friend and hid the wooden leg to stop his friend's lecturing?"

"I can't see why anyone would do that," the girl replies.

"Why not?" the voice up front asks.

"You tell us that writers make up stories. But this writer does not have a clue about handicaps or disabilities. And he is politically incorrect."

"Is that so?"

"Yes, I personally know someone who has a handicap and this person does not preach about it. In fact, this same person wants to be treated like everyone else and... plans to keep the handicap a secret. Is that so bad?"

"No, but why would that secret be bad?" the voice up front asks.

"Well, you once told us that our secrets could kill us."

"Maybe. Depends on the secret."

See Me

"RIGHT, LOOK AT ME," SHE REPLIES. "LOOK AT ME."

On the morning of the school dance, the girl stands shorter than most but taller in everything else.

She struts into the room with a brand new chest. Even her yellow blouse is not used to the stretching and the buttons strain, like tiny, weight-lifting faces. But the girl stares straight ahead, holding her head high and maintaining her rehearsed smile. One by one, other students notice that something is different about her. One boy points to the girl's face and circles his mouth with an index finger, as if to say her lips are not the same. Another girl gestures at her own hair and fans her fingers back and forth from her own ears and over her head, as if someone now has miracle hair. Another points to the girl's eyes and nods her head, while tapping on her own eyebrows. No one says anything about the girl's chest because maybe her sudden new breasts are like twin sisters needing time to get somewhere on their own.

Gradually, ever so gradually, the girl's left breast sags while her right breast stares straight ahead. More and more people notice... something. One student brings his hand to his mouth to hide his snickering and that reaction spreads to other boys. The girls look everywhere but at the fallen breast. A couple of other girls send text messages to the girl with the fallen breast. Another girl slips her a written note. The room is uneasy. The voice up front attributes it all to who the girls are.

Then the girl notices her own fallen breast and tissue hanging as a thick shirt-tail at her waist, her face a torch of apple red. She raises her arms and folds them at her chest. The tissue clump falls to the floor and is kicked from one desk to the next until a boy picks it up, examines it and then uses it to blow his nose. With her arms still at her chest, the girl holds up her right index finger and asks the voice up front if she can use the washroom.

"Go ahead," the voice up front replies. And the girl stands with her arms glued to her chest and quickly struts out of the room.

Later, when she returns, the girl still has her arms folded at her chest and everyone waits for her to drop her arms.

"I'm not feeling so well," she whispers to the voice up front.

"Do you need to go see the school nurse?" the voice up front asks.

"No, it's more than that," the girl replies.

"Or maybe you should go to the main office and phone your parents and tell them you're leaving school."

"Yeah, I better call my mom at her office and tell her I'm coming home because I'm... sick."

"Too bad. Is there anything I can do to help?" asks the voice up front, its words like velvet.

"Yes, there is. If anyone asks, can you say that I was not feeling right?"

"Of course. Unfortunately, you will miss the dance after school."

"Yeah, I was so, so ready for the dance."

"Get well soon."

"Thanks."

"See you tomorrow," the voice up front says.

"Right," she exhales, her breathing a slow leak of beauty.

Sparrows

IN THIS ROOM SPARROWS PERCH, LIKE NOTES ON SHEET MUSIC.
Their singing is mellow, earnest but not strained. No, their faces are easy with the world and swing back and forth under the maestro's moving wrists.

One boy, with blonde hair and green eyes, is dressed totally in black and sings alto. He is one of the tallest in the room and his eyes open and close, as if he is inhaling each musical note. His head swerves back and forth as he undoes the top button on his shirt in slow, slow motion. When looking closer at the boy, there is nothing coming out of his mouth except the sheer joy of song because singing might be his first tongue. All other chanting in the room is under his power. Meanwhile the maestro keeps watching the boy out of the corner of his eye and smiles a mouthful of piano-perfect teeth. "You make the song," the maestro exclaims pointing at the boy and the group is puzzled by the maestro's sudden outburst.

When the song's over, the tall boy gets up from his chair and asks for a drink break.

"Of course," says the maestro. "I wish my son were more like you."

Later, the boy returns while voices are in the middle of another piece of music and he stands by the door until the song's done before returning to his chair.

"I was taught to never ever interrupt the presence of a song," the boy says to the maestro.

"I can tell," replies the maestro. "And where did you learn that?"

"My parents listen to both classical and classic rock all the time. They live in two worlds!"

"Oh?"

The rest of the students pay close attention, as if being intrigued was their duty.

"For days after supper they played nothing but classical music from composers such as Mozart, Wagner, Chopin and Bizet and they hummed along to every piece. We also tried to guess the title of each composition. They showed us ways to remember who wrote what and how and when the music was written. "Classical music is something they know!" the boy says.

"That is amazing! I'll bet that not too many parents are like yours," the maestro replies with eyebrows rising to his forehead.

"Actually, it's quite easy to figure out," the boy says raising his own eyebrow. "They go back and forth."

"So that's the first world they live in?"

"Yes."

"Tell us about the second world," the maestro asks in a more than curious tone.

"Well, they play nothing but classic rock for days from artists such as The Rolling Stones or Tom Petty and the Heartbreakers. We learn everything about each song. All music has value according to my parents."

"Is that it?"

"After a couple of days, my parents play a mix of both classical and classic rock and we try to guess everything about each piece of music. If we get most of their questions correct, they give us money to buy any classical or rock and roll music that we want."

"Does mixing those two worlds confuse you at all?"

"Nope," the boy says. "Different types of music are actually made for each other, you know, like... ingredients for a recipe."

Life Is Not TV

"You couldn't understand me a couple of years ago," she says.

"Really," the voice up front says. "You sound good to me."

"When I came here from Mexico City, I was put into those English as a Second Language classes. I took class after class of E.S.L. and learned to listen, understand and do some speaking in English. We even started doing some reading and writing, but I wanted most was to lose my Mexican accent. I watched TV as much as I could. But then I started sounding like I was a regular in a sitcom or a contestant on a quiz show, but with a thick accent. People told me that life was not TV with an accent. And as you can tell, I still sound like someone from another place."

"You speak clearly enough for me," the voice up front replies in a neutral tone.

"Thank you! But my uncle, who has been here for a long time, says I still sound as if I just arrived in the trunk of a car a few nights ago. You know how some people joke about immigrants. Well, my uncle now thinks he is way better than any of us and he comes from Mexico City too."

"We were all immigrants at one time or another," answers the voice up front.

"Other people say that too, but it's more than that," the girl says.

"What more is there?"

"When some people hear me, they think I'm stupid too because of my accent, but I'm not!"

"True."

"But do I sound dumb?"

"No, not at all."

"The other day another person asked if anyone knew how a bird and a tree were the same. Most people said that a bird lives in a tree. I knew they were wrong, but did not say anything," the girl says with a quiet confidence.

"Why didn't you answer?" inquires the voice up front.

"I did not want to sound like I had nothing but a vast arid region between my ears. That other person must have noticed and she looked straight at me. Everyone grew quiet. In a loud Mexican-English voice I said: 'The bird and the tree are both alive.'"

"Makes sense to me," says the voice up front. "That's a higher level of thought."

"The other person said that too and everybody clapped for me," the girl added.

"Great. What you did is called abstract reasoning and only smart people can do that."

"Oh, I know I can think well."

"Good. That proves you really are smart, right?"

"Right."

"Ask your uncle about his own accent," the voice up front offers.

"Then... what?" the girl asks.

And her watered up eyes swim back and forth with hesitation.

Her Gender Tree

"Be prepared," the girl who could be at least a couple of years older than her real age and dressed completely in denim says. "My family tree is made of nothing but females. And I climb that tree each day just to be sure that everyone is where they should be."

"Really," replies the voice up front, "Then start at the bottom and work your way up."

"Grandma is the trunk for sure. One time I was over at her place with my mother and Grandma was watching Hockey Night in Canada game when Montreal was playing Toronto. She loves the Habs and hates those Leafs. When the Leafs iced the puck, she called them 'Lazy Pucksters' and, when the official skated quickly to the other end to retrieve the puck, she announced loudly that the linesman or ref must really need to go to the bathroom because he was skating so fast. She also brings chocolate-covered marshmallow cookies called Whippets every Sunday and warns us that, although the chocolate tastes good and the cookie part is fine, please moderate how you eat the middle ground, the marshmallow part, that softness, so as to not show any weaknesses. Grandma sure has a different way of being smart."

"What about your mother?" the voice up front asks.

"Mom can be fierce…tough and will challenge anyone who threatens our family. Plays in two bridge clubs. Likes her rye and water. Tries to stay up late reading Agatha Christie books so she does not have to go to bed at the same time as my father. At night I often hear him say: "Get to bed, Marie!" After several rye and waters, Mom will talk to her Agatha Christie books, as if murder mystery books rarely worry about bedtimes. She can be a big help to others too, like a couple of my older aunts who see my mom as their weekly angel and take-no-crap security guard. One time, when I was about six or seven, this older guy, from down the street, tried to pull my pants down and when my mother found out, she took care of him with a broom handle. No one on my street has touched my pants since... except me."

"And how about a couple of aunts? the voice up front asks.

"I have a few aunts but there are one or two who are the thickest tree branches. There's my Aunt Dot. She has eyes that want to hug...if they could. Cat's eyes are what they are. One time I ran home and when I got inside, I tripped over a carpet and knocked over a chair and the chair leg sliced through my mouth just below my bottom lip. After my chin was stitched up at the hospital, I remember most my Aunt Dot smiling so broadly at me, her eyes paying such close attention to my pain and the feather-like stroking of my face with her fingertips... that...that was better than anything.

Then, there's Aunt Darlene who is a hairdresser. Spends her money mostly on taxis and booze. When she drinks, she does not trust herself to ride the city bus. The last time she came over for a visit, my mother asked me to go outside and help Aunt Darlene out of the taxi and allow her to lean on me as I led her upstairs to our apartment. I remember one time when she thought I was the taxi driver and she gave me a two-dollar tip. One good thing, my aunt's hair always looks great but her head stinks like rotten eggs because of all the chemicals she uses. Her heart is the size of our kitchen table and she puts me in charge whenever she gets wishy-washy and I like that. Anyone can be fragile so she belongs in my tree, don't you think?"

"Okay now, wise person, do you know where you belong in the tree?" the voice up front asks, its eyes as wide open as can be.

"Not sure yet but… be prepared. I might surprise every-one."

Sorry

"WHEN DOES RESENTMENT FINALLY MELT?" THE VOICE UP FRONT asks itself.

Short, slim and completely transparent, the girl is a bottle of nectar-coloured pop which has been shaken far too often, but never opened.

Her father spends weekends in the bellies of beer bottles. There he relives the days when he sang in a rock n' roll band that did cover tunes. Most times he listens to a cassette tape of him singing a song about being stuck in the middle. The more he drinks, the better he thinks he sounds. The imaginary band members singing harmony sitting on either side of him become more real as the drinking takes effect. Something makes sound better. The father loves it all though and is soon singing the song to an imaginary audience of thousands in his basement.

Back then, he even looked like the lead singer in the real song. His hair was long forming its own alphabet on his neck and he laughed easily. The guys he played with all had great voices and could sing harmony to most songs. A case of beer was always there, but nobody ever drank too much.

Then the girl shouts: "Daddy... Daddy..." behind her father's voice. "I've given up trying to make sense of your cover tune." Meanwhile, after another beer, the father sings along even louder with his voice on the cassette. At the end of the song, he shouts: "I sound better than my voice on the cassette. I really do!"

The daughter wonders what would happen if the man on the cassette heard himself singing today because they are two different people. Would the cassette man be shocked? Would the two men have a beer together? Or would the man on the cassette simply shake his head and ask how he could help the today man?

When she approaches her father and taps him on the back, he turns, grabs her by the shoulders and shakes her in anger, his eyes almost spitting at her.

"Don't you ever scare me like that again!" he shouts.

"Why, why do you pretend so much?" she demands.

"You will never be a rock star. Never!"

"I...I am a star. My own star. Can't you see my shining? Now get the hell out of here!"

"No! Nobody is listening! Just you, your beer bottle and me."

Well, that does it! The glass of her skin explodes right there. There is nectar all over the floor, the walls, the cassette machine, and all over her father.

"Not true! Can't you see them? Can't you hear the rest of the band? Look... at the audience?" he mutters.

"I see a man sitting alone in a basement. I see a cassette machine. I see beer bottles. I hear my father singing the same song over and over. Stuck. Stuck in the middle. He sings along to his own voice, his younger voice. Can you bring back that younger voice? Can you?" she asks.

"I am sorry. I am so sorry I told you to get the hell out of here," the father answers, his voice sputtering while lowering his head.

"And I am sorry I told you that you'll never be a rock star," his daughter replies.

"But you are right," he says. "And I am sorry for being so sorry."

"When does resentment finally melt?" the voice up front asks itself.

Like The Water

"WILL YOU GET COLDER, LIKE THE WATER...WILL YOU?"

Three... two... one... and the bell rings several boys out the door and straight to the drinking fountain, as if only these boys knew about the simplicity of thirst. The girls, however, know the water can wait, and laugh at the boys' lack of impulse control. At the fountain, the boys slurp greedily and nudge each other out of the way, except for one boy named Allan. Even the girls pay more attention to him.

Allan stands aside by himself and lets everyone take a drink before him.

Noticeably shorter than most boys his age, Allan has a sloping forehead, small ear canals and yellow spots around his upward slanting, yet low-set eyes. Both his face and nose are flat. Allan spends part of his time in a regular room and the rest of the day in a special needs room half-way down the hallway. Not long ago, Allan's parents were told that their son would be in a regular classroom next year and this was called "inclusion".

Several boys gulp and swallow with water dripping down their chins and then move aside to let others have their turn. Allan leans against the wall licking his lips faster and faster. One girl whispers to another girl who whispers to another and within seconds, a path to the water fountain opens for Allan.

"Your turn… Allan," the shyest student in class suddenly announces. "You look very dry!"

The other students hardly ever hear this girl say a word in class and they wait there with their mouths nearly opened to the floor.

"Did you hear that?" asks a short girl in a navy blazer and who has more freckles than hair.

"Yeah, she never says a word," Peter with spiked brown hair, the colour of wheat proclaims and then laughs out loud.

Then Allan shuffles his way by the girls and says: "Thank you!"

Everyone, including the boys, study Allan drinking from the fountain. He drinks and drinks until the same shyest girl says: "Allan, you're going to drown!"

Allan lifts his head from the fountain and then pats his stomach. Water beads trickle down his chin and onto his T-shirt. His hands drip as he throws them into the air, like wet flowers.

"See, I drink too. And next year my mommy and daddy said I will be just like all of you. I will run to the water fountain, like the boys. I will drink water just like all of you. I will let others drink too. Only the temperature of the water will drop the more it is used. Isn't that something? I will not be cold, like the running water. No, I won't. What about all of you? Will you be different with me?"

Living Forever

"LAST NIGHT I SAW AN OLDER ITALIAN MOVIE MADE IN THE MID 1960's. A young woman was sitting on the back of a fast-moving motor scooter in Rome. She looked like she was glued to the man she was holding onto," says a short, yellow-haired boy with eye-glasses as wide as a car windshield. "The boyfriend was dressed in black leather with a blood-red scarf flowing from his neck. She also wore black leather from her head to her toes, her long, shiny chestnut hair weaving through the sunlit streets of Rome. The two of them looked like a single body of black leather on that scooter. Neither one of them was wearing a helmet. Both laughed wildly, as if speeding and possible death were a joke. I am not sure why people laugh at the blow that kills?"

"I don't know," the voice up front replies. "Maybe, when you're young, you think you'll live forever."

"I'm young but I sure don't want to live forever," the boy says. "I'm also afraid of dying."

"I suppose most of us fear death in one way or another," says the voice up front. "Tell me more about the film."

"We never hear a single word from the leather couple on the scooter. There is one main character in the story and we find out early that she wants something but some kind of obstacle always gets in her way. There is tension, of course, because she cannot get what she wants...you know, the usual

49

kind of story. I suppose it does not matter if it is a woman or a man. Someone always wants or needs something in a story."

"True, but what about the couple on the scooter?"

"Nothing. They just kept reappearing in the background over and over but they never said a word. What a long scooter ride for a two-hour movie!"

"Did the scooter couple have to say or do something… anything for the story to make sense?" the voice up front asks.

"I don't know for sure but why were they in the movie in the first place?"

Outside the room, broken portions of cloud try unsuccessfully to fit together, like lost puzzle pieces and their efforts confuse the sun. A passing ambulance with its siren blaring demands that all vehicles move over. This gives the voice up front time to contemplate what to say next.

"Different cultures have different ways to tell a story and maybe the couple on that scooter were there for a reason. For example, what if that main character was looking for a lover dressed in black leather?"

"Could be. She seemed lonely in the movie but it was unclear what or who she was looking for."

"Maybe, the film had an open ending and the viewer had to imagine how the story ends," the voice up front suggests.

"But I wanted the ending to be clear so I could put the story to bed, like a kid getting ready for sleep. I like to move on after seeing a film."

"Okay, but many times stories are not all black and white. Occasionally we need to figure it out ourselves."

"There was nothing gray about that couple on the scooter. They wanted each other. Period."

Outside the cloudless sky is now distinctly blue and the sun is beaming. Traffic is light. There are no sirens. The boy with the extra-wide eyeglasses looks out the window, as if waiting for the slightest change in the ending of his movie.

The Smell of a Prince

"REMEMBER TO TELL US WHAT REALLY HAPPENED WHEN WE COME back after Christmas."

Three weeks before Christmas, coins are secretly passed from one hand to the next until the money eventually gathers in the hands of the tall, studious girl at the back of the room. She is the tallest and has teak brown eyes and such long, thick, curly, brown hair, the colour of straw that another girl once teased that a children's story could be written about her hair.

"Maybe, you could toss your long hair out the window and a handsome prince might climb up and rescue you," a girl dressed in all yellow says.

"Ah, I don't need rescuing and I don't live in a tower," the girl jokes back. "Too many steps."

"Are you too old to pretend?" the voice up front asks.

"No, but I don't believe in those fairy tale princes!"

"Okay" the voice says.

"They're not real to me," she replies. "Never have been."

Little did the voice up front know that the same girl with the long hair was also collecting money from everyone to buy the voice up front a gift.

A few days before Christmas break, it is decided that the group will use the money to buy the voice up front several bottles of aftershave lotion and/or cologne.

"Surely, the voice up front must see those ads," someone says.

"The ads tell men to splash it all over and they say that it is a favourite for Christmas stockings. Bet even movie stars use those aftershaves and colognes," offers another.

"Yeah, one aftershave comes in different scents and is the mark of a... man, especially if he's wearing an open shirt and carrying a bottle of wine," a third boy with slicked back hair mentions.

A fourth says, "What about this other cologne? The ads say that a generous splash is considered a sure-fire way to attract women. I saw a sign the other day that showed a man using martial arts to fight off an incredibly fit woman who just loved the smell. Imagine that! We better go shopping soon."

"Good idea," says the brown-haired girl. "Not much time left before Christmas. But I wonder how many women who use perfume need to fight off men?"

A few days before the Christmas break, the girl in charge goes shopping with one other girl and two boys. The four of them hurry into a nearby store. They decide to buy three bottles of aftershave and cologne because they figure it might somehow improve the holidays for the voice up front.

On the last day before Christmas break when the voice opens his gifts, he jokingly says: "I feel like a prince with all these sweet-smelling gifts. Thank you everyone."

"Hold on. Even if princes exist, would they avoid women? Women might avoid princes," the long-haired girl declares with confidence. "Because some princes think they are entitled and that annoys women."

"Then why all this aftershave and cologne? Didn't you say that princes were not real? And you know, even a make-believe prince can have a sense of humour," says the voice up front.

"Maybe, but I thought you would just like to smell good. Like most people, at this time of the year," answers the girl.

"Sure, why not. It is the season to smell so good."

"Remember to tell us what happened when we come back after Christmas."

The Aroma of Lies

"Not sure," replies the voice up front. "But you'll find out soon enough."

The boy has a noticeable belly and with sad, green eyes waddles up to the voice up front after everyone has left.

"Can I talk to you?" the boy asks.

"Of course, pull up a chair," the voice up front says. "What's up?"

Everything smells stuffy from all the bodies of the day. The voice up front loosens its tie and removes its jacket. Even the sun pouring in from the windows hesitates to brighten up the room, as if something is not quite right about these four walls.

"I wrote an anonymous letter to another voice up front that I had last year. I just hated that voice. She was a mumbling bully and made me feel so small. She once asked me where I am hiding my real self. That was mean. Imagine a voice asking that question. I was afraid of her. I was afraid of what I wanted to do to her. Other boys also felt the same way but never any girls. I have been keeping my anger inside for nearly a year now until I exploded on paper a couple of weeks ago. But I am still paying for that letter. I feel so bad. It was the wrong thing to do. But if I apologize to her, she will find ways to make my life totally miserable. That I know for sure."

"Yes, I overheard the voice you're talking about, sharing the letter with someone in the staffroom," says the voice up front.

"Really?"

"She was very upset. She even wondered if it might be a colleague who wrote the nasty letter because many of the other voices are unsure about her."

"No big secret. Most of us notice that other voices do not want to be around her because they only talk or joke around with each other and never with her in the hallways. I have trouble sleeping. I feel so guilty. I lie to myself saying she deserved it so I can feel better. I need some truth?" the boy asks.

Even with the wide-open door and open windows, the room still smells stagnant, stale. The voice up front squirms slightly in its chair. Why does the room feel so dull, so sluggish?

"I can't stop telling myself how she will do me permanent damage if I apologize to her. Right now, I will wait until she dies and then maybe ask for forgiveness near her coffin at the funeral."

"There may be another way to solve this if a direct amend could cause more harm than good," says the voice up front.

Then a glow suddenly reaches across the room, as if the arms of sun were ready to do what they do best. That warmth is followed by a cool breeze causing both the boy and the voice up front to inhale and exhale the freshness deeply, like the medicine in mountain air.

"Perhaps, for now anyway, you can make an amend to her by substitution. Can you do the right thing by helping someone else?"

"Maybe I can help out at that senior's residence down the street from here and keep helping until I feel better about the letter."

"That's a good start," the voice up front says.

"Does that get me off the hook for the letter?"

"Not sure," the voice up front replies. "But you'll find out soon enough."

And It All Started So Small – ONE

(For Danny H.)

"It all started so small," I tell the voice up front.

It looks like I caught the voice unprepared because it was getting ready to leave the room, but my words need somewhere else to go.

"Suddenly, a word would be hard for my father to say. At the time, we all thought that he was just tired because of his job. My mother explained that he worked for the railway and often negotiated many big dollar contracts at the same time with suppliers and he told my mom he saw himself as a money juggler.

Even though my father was paid very good money, he wanted us all to go to the local school near our home instead of some fancy private school. He reminded us that sure, a sound education begins with a roof over our heads but if we wanted to learn to dance with life, we had to start on the streets.

Soon my father had trouble with tingling in his right hand and then his entire right arm would not work right. He could not lift anything, even my two little sisters. Later he struggled going upstairs. Then my dad began mumbling more and sometimes stumbled over his feet or fell to the floor. Doctors sent him to specialists in Edmonton and Montreal and finally everyone said that my father had ALS or Lou Gehrig's disease. I mean he can still see, smell, taste, hear, touch and go to the bathroom, like everyone else. The hardest part... he has his brain working just fine but he looks like he is trapped inside his body. For a while, he ate regular food, like spaghetti, but had to stay away from things like grapes, which made him choke. Now he is fed mostly by an IV tube and then a bottle on one of those tall metal stands. At first, he used a cane, then a walker, but now... mostly this special electric wheelchair.

Last night we celebrated their wedding anniversary at a small hall and about forty people showed up to help celebrate. My father and mother danced to *Blue Hawaii* sung by a fake Elvis. Halfway through the song, my father had to lean on my mother. When Elvis moved on to *Jailhouse Rock*, my father had to be held up in my mother's arms, like a rag doll doing the jitterbug. Then he started sobbing in her arms and some guests moved onto the dance floor to form a protective circle around my parents. When the pretend Elvis noticed my father bawling, he nudged his black wig back and forth on his bald head, as if the song were about my father alone. Some people patted my father on the back. Others stroked his hair. Still others hugged both of my parents and danced with them. The circle got tighter. Elvis kept singing. Before long nearly every single person in the room was on the dance floor and took turns in the protective circle. Eyes watered up everywhere but the *Jailhouse Rock* circle remained intact, as if only tears could lubricate the circle action. I watched my father wipe his pain on my mother's chest. And my mother -well she just kept smiling that strong smile of hers and kissed as much hope as she could into my father's hair. Then every man, woman and child in the room took turns burrowing into the circle and pressed their lips on my father's head. So...so many people wanted to protect my father from the idea that he might last for one more year, or two, as if they wanted his chest muscles to never stop working. And he had trouble moving his arms, legs and skinny body on the dance floor. What else do all these people want? And when will that fake Elvis stop singing? When? I mean, I stayed seated at our table because I was all cried out and someone... had to keep an eye on my two little sisters.

TWO

"IT HASN'T GONE AWAY," I CONTINUE TELLING THE VOICE UP front as the sun is slowly pulled down from the sky, like a window blind. "My two little sisters are talking less and less and are becoming strangers to each other."

"Your father?" asks the voice up front. "How's he doing?"

"Gotten worse. The other night when everyone went for groceries, I wanted to stay home and watch over him, even though there was a home care person there to do all the work. My mother tried everything to get me out of the house, but I would not budge. She knew."

"So how did it go?"

"Well, my father now has a dot on his forehead and he points his head to letters on his iPad. Letter by letter he tells us what he wants. And the computer does the rest. Aside from my father's grunting and moaning, that is the only way he can communicate with us now."

"Must be hard for you to watch," says the voice up front.

"Not as hard as watching him in his ceiling sling."

"Ceiling sling?"

"Yes, our house now looks like a huge hospital ward with machines all over the place to help the home care people with my dad. One of the machines has a hoist and sling attached to it. The home care person, and sometimes my mom too, push a button after attaching the sling to my father's body. Then he is lifted into the air so adjustments can be made. You should see what he looks like huddled in this sling. His shoulders are squished together almost to his cheeks. His eyes move further into his head, as if they are searching for new sockets. Now remember, only his brain has not changed one bit and he is watching the rest of his body melt from the inside out. When my father stares down at me, he looks like a fetus I saw last week in a science book. I would love to know what he is really thinking and feeling."

"Now that would tell you a lot for sure," says the voice up front.

"Yeah, there's only so much he can say with that dot on his forehead."

"What would you ask your father?"

"I want to know about the inside of his brain. Is he trying to maybe go back inside his mother and start his life all over again without the Lou Gehrig's disease? He just looks so, so scared.

"I can think of many reasons why he's afraid," the voice up front says.

"Maybe his eyes want to run away somewhere."

"What about your mom?" asks the voice up front.

"When everyone got home with the groceries, my mom took one look at my dad and dropped everything on the kitchen floor. Then she shoved her fist at the ceiling and yelled: 'I didn't marry this man so I'd have to take care of him in a freaking sling!'

"Boy, did she ever feel bad for saying that!"

"Your mom is only human. She must also be very scared," replies the voice up front. "No wonder she felt so bad. Often when people are afraid, they get angry and lash out."

"Okay, but she's not the one watching herself die hanging in the air like that."

"Must be so hard on your mom. Perhaps she would love to exchange places with your dad. Who knows?"

"What? What do you mean?"

"Ask your mom how you can help?"

"I do not...do not want to help. I want to hear my dad
talk about the Montreal Canadiens, the Habs...he loves them.
I want to hear him tell jokes as he cooks. I want him to play
his drums and cribbage. I want him out... of that goddam
sling!" the boy says. "Now!"

THREE

"Sorry to hear about your dad's passing," the voice up front says to me privately some time later.

My thirteen-year-old brain is going on twenty-three an uncle of mine told me a few days ago. The rest of the day goes by so slowly that I feel myself reaching my mid-twenties before noon. I am growing up to meet death.

After everyone has gone, I get up to leave and my body is heavier than it has been all day.

"Still want to talk?" the voice up front almost murmurs as I walk by.

I grab a chair in slow motion and inch it closer to the voice up front.

"Yeah, he is gone. Dead. Really dead. There was a celebration of his life the day before the funeral. You should have seen all the people there telling stories and jokes about my father. Many teased him about how careful he was with money and that he could hear a five-dollar hit the snow. My father's boss mentioned that my dad was a ruthless negotiator, like a bulldog, and she appreciated both his tenacity and the gleam in his eye after scoring a big deal with a supplier.

A close friend, who is a fair bit older than my father, told of how he took my dad to a Flames-Canadiens hockey game at the Saddledome. A few of my father's hockey buddies met them before the game and had a burger and beer with them. The close friend talked about how my dad's buddies teased

him about not being able to speak up. Not that funny but
you know how guys are. Each guy hugged my father in that
awkward way that men do. They knew he did not have much
longer. They knew. The close friend had tried to get them both
into the Montreal Canadiens dressing-room before the game
but it did not work out because my dad was at that stage when
he needed the help of a walker but was not ready for a wheelchair. When my dad took pictures of the game action with
his tablet, an usher rushed up and said picture-taking was not
allowed. 'Leave him alone. He has ALS,' the good friend said.

The usher apologized. My dad even took a picture of the
usher and thanked him by tapping on his chest right where
his heart is or was."

"He was lucky to have so many good friends. He must
have been a good guy, your dad," the voice up front says.

"Yeah, but I wish I had not been so quiet and sitting
alone on that day before the funeral. I was storing up all the
things I wanted to tell my father, but I was silent…nothing.
Maybe, what I wanted to say all comes from my own darkness
and he comes from the light. He was ready to pass on to the
side of the angels, like my mother says, but I do not believe
in angels, do you?"

"Depends."

"Depends on what?" I ask.

"Did you help carry your father's casket on the day of
the funeral?"

"What does that have to do with angels? No, I did not
help with the casket. I had too much to say to my dad before
he went to those… angels. I was also busy helping my mom
comfort my two younger sisters who kept crying during and
after the funeral. I could not cry. Nope. I needed to be stron-
ger than those… pretend angels. Bullshit!"

"What do you want to say to your father?"

"Oh, I am saving all that up for when I take his ashes
for a ride on my bike. And those angels… they better not be
listening or I will set their wings on fire."

It all started so small.

Recipe (for Paul Rivard)

THE BOY WITH THE RAZOR-SHORT, BRUSH CUT SITS SO QUIETLY, SO motionless that his thoughts can be seen through his scalp.

Meanwhile the voice up front moves down the rows checking to see that last night's work is done. On the boy's scalp, it shows him exploding with laughter yesterday evening. He is watching two Marx Brothers movies, *A DAY AT THE RACES* and *THE BIG STORE,* one after the other, with his father who is seated in an old stuffed armchair and the boy plops himself on the carpet between his father's feet. The films make the father's laughter rumble through his torso, arms and legs and downward towards his son.

"Having a good time?" asks the father.

"Yeah, they're hilarious!" replies the son.

"Hilarious? Never heard you use that word before. Anyhow, I just want to be sure you never forget how to laugh," the father says to the son. "Laughter always has a place. And tonight, do not worry about your school work. I will write you a note."

The boy's scalp shows that he did not have time for school work last night because purposeful laughter took over his life. Later, the son looks up at his father and asks, "What about the note for tomorrow?"

"Oh, right. I will get to it when *THE BIG STORE* is done."

When the second film is over and both the father and son have numbed bellies, the son stumbles off to bed still holding his sides. Then the father goes into the kitchen, takes out a sheet of paper and sits at the kitchen table. His note says:

"Dear Voice Up Front, I know homework is important. However, my son did not do any last night because I was exposing him to the gift of laughter, something I had been planning for many days. After all, surely you know, if a kid cannot recognize a gift and the joy that goes with it, he will never be ready to learn anything. So, can you please keep a close eye on my son and tell me if he learned better today? Please write back. Thank you for your time."

Then the father folds the note, slides it into an envelope and tucks the envelope into his son's brown paper lunch bag.

The next day the boy gives the note to the voice up front. Later, when the voice approaches him and notices the story through his scalp, the voice up front says: "Aha! I bet I can guess what this letter says before reading it. Bet you are going to have the best day ever. See me later today and I will reply to your dad."

"How does the voice up front know?" the boy asks himself while looking at the floor. "How?"

All day long, the boy soaks up anything and everything until his brain throbs under his scalp. By the end of the afternoon, the voice up front walks towards the boy to give him the note for his father.

At home, the boy's scalp shows both he and his father hovering over the kitchen table and reading the voice up front's note. It reads: "Dear Sir, your son was spectacular today. He could not get enough of what we did and his brain grew legs of its own. Would it be possible for you to take some time off work and visit us in the future? We both know that not everything is a joke but perhaps you could show us what laughter did to your son. You will not need a note from

anyone either. That is a joke. Ha! Ha! And would you especially explain the difference between a first and a last laugh
because we are all curious about how humour and joy starts
and ends? Thank you."

Hand

THE BOY'S HAND HAS A LIFE OF ITS OWN.

"Touch me one more time like that and I'll chop off your hand!" mutters the girl who could be older than her age of thirteen.

The boy behind her looks downward and pretends to be looking for something. He searches everywhere while ignoring the girl in front of him. Then the boy notices a blue ballpoint pen on the floor near the window and moves away from the girl. He bends over to retrieve the pen and at the same time, hears the girl say: "Stop looking like you do not know what you are doing! It was your hand that touched me, wasn't it?"

The voice up front moves quickly towards the back of the room and asks both girl and boy to step outside. The boy stuffs the blue ballpoint pen into his shirt pocket and follows the girl and the voice up front out the door into the hallway.

"Okay, what's going on with you two?" the voice up front demands.

"He touched me where he wasn't supposed to!" the girl exclaims pointing to the back pocket of her jeans.

"Not true," says the boy. "I was standing behind her waiting to move so I could get to my desk. Nothing more."

"Liar! I felt your hand on my butt. Your fingers did not just brush me by accident."

"Look, I did not touch you. You must have imagined it."

"Here, imagine this."

And the girl reaches around the boy, grabs him by the back pocket and spins him around.

"Does that feel imagined?" she asks, her eyes spitting thumbtacks at him.

"Okay. Okay. Enough!" the voice up front interrupts. "People do not imagine that kind of thing. I want you to apologize to her. Now! Next time that happens, I'm taking you down to the Principal after class so she knows what happened. From now on, keep your touching to yourself! Is that clear?"

"Sorry," says the boy.

The girl walks back into the room, her head held high and slams a fist on her desk.

"Remember what I said," says the voice up front. "Now, let's go back inside and complete what we're doing."

When the class is over, everyone rises from their desks and begins moving out of the room. The boy and the girl happen to sweep by each other. Suddenly she turns to him and punches him hard in that place between his nose and mouth. Blood pours down the boy's chin. Students back themselves to the walls expecting a major fight. After she grabs his face with her right hand, the boy tries to knee the girl in her groin, but she catches his leg with her left hand and pulls him to the floor. Pinning both his shoulders to the floor with her knees, the girl says: "I warned you," and then slaps his bloodied face with her left hand making the blood splatter onto the legs and shoes of onlookers.

The voice up front quickly pulls them apart and hauls them both downstairs.

"I warned you," the girl shouts at the bloodied boy.

The boy's hand has a life of its own.

Dirt Road

"Simple. I need to find a way off my dirt road."

Quite slim and tall for his age, the boy looks older, but he had hoped all the pimples and changes would start later. Much later. Yes, the boy's skin belongs on the bones of someone else.

His mind is sharp though. The boy remembers the first time he knew about being alone on a dirt road. Hard to believe but he was four. So many relatives squeezed his cheeks and picked him up in their arms. He especially hated the cheek-grabbing, the pinching pain. Eventually his sore cheeks pushed him back into himself and he found ways to avoid face to face contact with relatives. He hid mostly behind his mother and sometimes his father. Or the boy pretended to be busily building something. Or he hid under the darkness of his bed. But the relatives ignored his avoidance strategies and tried other ways like hugging, kissing and pats on the head.

"That boy...that boy is special," one aunt mentioned after a Thanksgiving gathering.

"Yeah, people will pay attention to him," said an uncle last Christmas.

"Wait till he becomes a real teenager," a much older cousin announced to everyone after one of the boy's birthday parties. "There'll be no stopping him!"

For some reason, the boy remembers every word that was ever said about him since he was four years of age and his

67

time alone on that dirt road. However, there are days when he wishes his memory was porous.

Only now is he starting to care so much.

For some reason, the boy trusts the voice up front because the voice seems unconcerned about being special, having blemishes or excessive height, or being skinny. He likes talking to the voice up front, especially after hearing the voice talk about being extra tall and boney for its age and the start of a bad complexion when it was thirteen. And the voice up front also mentioned that it felt like being lost on a lonely road, a dirt road.

"It is strange. You know, I felt like that kid who was born to not fit in anywhere. My face even looked like a dirt road. My skin was not my own. I even wanted to trade in my body," the voice up front said while discussing the story they had read about a homeless boy. "Some of my buddies felt the same way, but I didn't find out until we were all much older."

When the class ends and everyone, except the boy, moves on to their next room, the voice up front looks up and says, "Oh, you are still here. Is there something you want to discuss?"

"Kind of," the boy says.

"What can I do for you?" the voice up front asks.

"Simple. I need to find a way off my dirt road."

The Plea

AFTER THE ROOM EMPTIES, A GREEN-EYED GIRL APPROACHES THE voice up front and says, "My father... is always right. Pride. It is in his bones."

"Oh, have you... tried talking with him?" the voice up front asks shuffling from one foot to the next.

"Are you crazy? Never. And because he is so overweight, he looks hilarious with that big, black Nike mark on his sweater; makes him look like something checked off on a grocery list at a fat food store. Nothing but designer clothes for him. Often, he acts like a big-shot but I think he is scared... of something. Normal conversations he knows nothing about. Comes from a poor background, but wants everyone to think he is rich. Why does he pretend? Why? What's worst is that he knows more about being critical than being curious. Whenever he talks, he mumbles, as if he is hiding...something. I think he is afraid of lots of things. I can tell. I can tell because... most people do not want to be around him. According to him, anyone who tries to look better has too much vanity. I need to trade him in. I want... a truthful, brave father."

"Okay, okay, but what about your mother?" the voice up front asks. "Surely, you can talk to her."

"Well, she comes from Scotland. Acts like she just got here. Says she came to Canada when she was too old, a teenager, I think, and she has never been at home here. She still

69

has that accent. She cannot make decisions. She pouts. She whines. The weather is too cold or too hot. If someone buys a new stove, she wants a new stove. So weird how my father thinks and acts for her; she is totally his puppet. One time she asked my father to approve which bra to buy. They do not have any real friends. My mother must be frightened too…of something. I need to trade her in. I mean I want…an honest, courageous mother."

"Maybe, your mom is just tired. Perhaps she is lonely, like lots of people. And maybe your father does not know any better. See me again tomorrow after class."

The following day, after the room clears, the voice up front, calmly says:

"There must be something good you can say about your parents. Maybe their childhoods were terrible. Who knows? Could be lots of reasons. Nobody is perfect."

"I try to understand them," the girl answers. " Everyone says that I can see right through people. I know I have a good brain and, I am not sure but… maybe I see too much."

"You are doing very well in school," offers the voice up front. "And you will be graduating soon too. Can you try to say something positive about your parents?"

"Well, my father can be kind. He is dependable, loyal. And my mother works hard, likes to read, like I do, and she has moments of being smart too."

"Would you like me to have a talk with your parents?"

"No, no, just watch and listen when they come for interviews and let me know if you think I need new parents."

"But I do not live with your family so how can I know? Besides, I am no expert. No one is," the voice up front says and then clears its throat.

"But you know me," says the girl. "That should be enough."

The voice up front leans back in its chair, stares wide-eyed at the ceiling with its hands locked behind its head and exhales slowly from partially-puffed up cheeks, as if its face were being punctured by the smallest of doubts.

Click

SILLY IS NOT THE SAME FOR EVERYONE.

Clusters of faces suddenly bunch together to prepare for the camera. They all aim their looks without much coaching before the photo is even taken. Fingers extend in V shaped clumps of two, both in front of faces and behind heads. The occasional fist is thrust upwards in a victory salute. There are stretched smiles, small, unsure grins and faces of wide-open, pretend shock. Some show too many teeth. Two or three tongues stab the air. A couple have only clenched mouths. When told that the pictures should be back in one week, nearly everyone vows to be the first in the room that day.

Standing by himself, over by the door, is a boy born into shyness. Shorter than everyone else, his clothes are too big on him and sag like tired skins. His hair has a ditch-like part down the middle of his head and he might be daring someone to dig into his head to have a closer look. And his denim blue eyes create a new dance, as if they are knitting a protective wall of wire in front of him. When asked by the voice up front to join the group, the boy says," I hate having my picture taken!"

"Why is that?" the voice up front asks.

"I just do," replies the boy.

"Well, please stay here. I need to ask you something afterwards."

"Okay."

After everyone leaves, the voice up front asks, "How's everything going?"

"Couldn't be better," the boy replies, his voice a rehearsed song.

"Good. Is there a problem with someone taking your picture?"

The boy drops his head to his chest, like a bag of nectarines and then folds his fingers into a tent on his stomach. His feet move up and down as he clears his throat. Then the boy lifts his head and looks directly at the voice up front.

"Do you have to know?" asks the boy.

"Nope, you do not have to say anything. Surely there are other people who do not like being photographed too. Are you okay?"

"I am fine. Time for me to go home."

As the boy walks towards the doorway, he turns and looks back at the voice up front with a knotted crease between his eyes and then pulls out an imaginary camera from his jacket. The boy clicks once, twice, three times. Then he adjusts the lens for a close-up and snaps again and again. After, the boy turns the invisible camera sideways and clicks one more time. Finally, he points at the voice up front and says, "Smile! Can you smile and talk at the same time? Click! Click! Click!" and disappears into the hallway.

Days later, when the pictures arrive, the voice up front is anxious to show off the photos. The boy who hates having his picture taken stands back from the group clustered around the voice up front's desk. After the unvarnished responses, the wide-eyed joy from everyone else, one by one each turns to stare at the boy over by the door, their gazing becoming a wall of eyes. Someone says, "Hey, come and have a look. Too bad you missed out on a chance to be a bit silly."

"Being foolish never makes me laugh much," answers the boy.

"That's okay," the voice up front replies. "Silly is not the same for everyone."

Knuckles

"DON'T GO NOWHERE WITHOUT 'EM," THE MAN SAYS.

The intercom buzzes to signal the start of another ten-minute segment.

The voice up front watches the approaching father and offers him a chair. Stiff in his tight-fitting, white shirt, blue necktie and clinging navy suit, the father looks as if he is a working-class guy forced to wear a new skin just for tonight. Then the man slowly lowers himself into the chair across from the voice up front.

"Thanks for coming," the voice up front says.

"I'm here," says the father. "How is my kid doing?"

Then the voice up front reviews achievement, stresses the positives and asks the father if he had any questions or concerns.

"Okay, my boy is doing well. What about his behaviour. Do YOU have any concerns?"

"Not really. Why do you ask?"

"Because my son can be a big pain in the ass at home. No matter what I do, he hates me. And I let him know when he has crossed the line. Sometimes I need to rap him on the head with my knuckles when he misbehaves. Know what I mean?"

"Sort of," replies the voice up front. "Knuckles."

"Like this." And the father raps his knuckles on the voice up front's desk.

"That must hurt you more than him."

"Nope, it does the trick," says the father. "I think."

"Your son certainly behaves here. In my opinion, kids generally misbehave because they are not motivated, or need attention or require firmer limits," the voice up front says. "Maybe there are other reasons too."

"My knuckles cover all three, wouldn't you say? He sure gets motivated quickly. I pay attention to him and my boy knows real fast that he has reached the limit!"

"Right," replies the voice up front. "Does his behaviour change after that?"

"For a short time anyway. But after he rubs away his pain, he starts all over again."

"Do you want to discuss this further?"

"Are you're a knuckle expert," he asks the voice up front.

Suddenly, there is a loud rapping at the door and hallway voices grow quiet. The intercom buzzes.

"No, I am not an expert but we are running out of time. Can we make another appointment for say the twenty-third, next week at 4:30 pm?"

"Sure, let me write it down on my pack of smokes: School appointment, twenty-third at 4:30pm. Done."

"Bring your knuckles," the voice up front says.

"Don't go anywhere without 'em," the man replies.

LAST DAYS

Comb on the Range

As the bathroom door squeaks open and closes, the hallway becomes an attentive ear.

Nearly hidden behind the last marble partition for the urine stalls by a sink, a tall, eminent boy of seventeen sheathes his comb when he sees the voice up front enter and then washes his hands so thoroughly, as if the hands are holding a secret. In his western boots and leather vest, he is the prominent dude, a cowboy at home on the range. With eyes focussed on soaping his fingers and hands, the boy curls himself into the sink and stares at the noise of the rushing water swirling down the drain.

Perhaps he is alone at a campfire, heating beans in a skillet because his pot is no longer useful for any cooking. Or maybe he prepares everything in that skillet. In his wet left hand is a metal cup of steaming coffee from which he takes a sip and then he carefully places the cup on the corner of the sink so he can dry his hands. Is this a washroom or the range? Twice tugging paper towels from the dispenser, the boy makes paper noises that came from rubbing and drying as he balls up the brown wetness. Then his fingers flip open the steel flap of the garbage can and drops it all in with the other garbage. Done. He studies himself in the mirror one more time and is dissatisfied with his hair. Out comes his comb again. He parts, pats, fluffs, puffs and combs, twisting his gaze from side to side. Tilting his head to the left and then to the right, he smiles, shrugs and throws his hands, palms stretching outward to the walls, as if preparing to go on stage.

What does he do to look and feel just right when he is alone on the prairie with no mirror, no urinals, no sink, no soap or paper towel dispensers? His comb must have a vision of its own when not stuffed into the right back pocket of his blue jeans. Maybe the boy hums his hair to sleep around the campfire, the flickering flames also inviting the moon for a sleepover. The crackling sounds of the burning wood are his only audience. Wolves try to unsettle his hair with their sudden howling, their piercing cries. Snakes swallow as much of his song as possible while ignoring the cold because they may now be thirsty for the boy's blood. And the moon remains wide-open yellow and motionless no matter how off-key the boy sounds.

Soon he pats his head ever so gently and checks it all out in various black mirrors of night, but no one looks back at him. But he keeps trying to find just one mirror that works. And there it is, just below a corner of sky surrounded by stars, is a small black stream shining in the night. Right then, the boy pulls out his comb again and starts with the parting, the patting, the fluffing, the puffing. He likes what he sees, even though his eyes may distrust the night. Two thin clouds, following one another, float across the sky and almost cut the moon into slices, like a lemon pie. A huge mountain in the background falls asleep in the blackness and seems comfortable with its own giant lack of pride. And the quiet wind gradually turns the pages of night, one black sheet at a time.

Back in the washroom, the boy walks by the voice up front and nods politely.

"I never see you in here," says the boy.

"I never come in here," replies the voice up front. "We have our own washroom. But occasionally we check the washrooms as part of our job."

"I get it," the boy says.

When the voice up front turns to watch him exit, the boy pats the comb in his back pocket and lifts the collar on his shirt, as if the world were waiting to interview him in the hallway.

As the bathroom door squeaks open and closes, the hall-way becomes an attentive ear.

Stopping The Clock

Is the clock on the wall attached to a bomb?

Friday afternoon and more and more of the long, tall bodies in chairs become giant second hands themselves. After each click of the clock, another body squirms and shuffles in a seat. The voice up front peeks at the clock and keeps going, knowing full well that time is simply being filled until the end of the day. With a few minutes remaining, the voice up front stops and assigns work to be completed over the weekend. Lots of time to cover before the bell rings, meaning lots more twisting and turning. But the voice up front knows that if it continues, time will stop and a Friday afternoon will erupt into something,

One by one, all but one face joins a ripple effect of eyes focussed on the clock after copying the assignment.

Over by the window, a short, newly dyed, redheaded girl dressed in blood-red jeans, a white, long-sleeved blouse and a baggy black wool vest, bends over her work. Her face, the colour of a freshly-washed, white bedsheet, rests on her hands. No one appears to wonder about her except for the voice up front. The bell rings and bodies almost fling themselves out of the room.

"Can I help you with something?" the voice up front asks the girl after the room empties.

"I want it to stop," she says lifting her moon shaped face towards the window.

"What do you want stopped?"

"The clock," she answers while brushing her braided hair back over her right ear.

"Why is that?"

"So the baby inside me will stop growing. I figure if the clock stops, then maybe the baby inside me will stop getting bigger."

"Come up here for a moment, please. And how long have you been expecting?" the voice up front asks in a voice as gentle as a three-year-old child offering make-believe tea.

"About three and a half months," replies the girl. "Can't you tell? Everyone knows."

"Not me. What are your plans?" the voice inquires.

"Not sure. I just want that clock on the wall to stop ticking so I can have more time to think about what to do. Can you get rid of the clock or make it stop for a while somehow, please?"

"I don't think that's possible."

"Why can't it stop just for me?" the girl pleads.

"Unfortunately, it doesn't stop for anyone," says the voice up front.

"Not fair. I am only seventeen almost eighteen!"

"Must be tough."

"I don't need your pity."

"Right. Is there anything I can do to help?" the voice up front asks breathing in some calmness.

"Nope, if you can't give me more time, there's nothing you can do!"

"Take care and have a safe weekend," the voice up front says.

"How do I take care... of time?" the girl asks as she points at the clock on her way out. "And what's so safe about this?" she mutters while patting her belly?"

Is the clock on the wall attached to a bomb?

Shakespeare And Motorcycles

"IMAGINE," THE VOICE UP FRONT SAYS. "IMAGINE THAT."

There they sit slumped and bewildered. Some throw up their hands, as if offering their confusion to a shadowy literary power hanging from the ceiling. Others scratch their heads with their brains sifting through every word. Still others mumble to themselves, as if Shakespeare were a newly discovered insect emerging from the earth after a volcanic eruption.

"Some people say that William Shakespeare is the greatest writer of all time. Every writer after him is an imitator. Shakespeare knew more about human behaviour than anyone. The play we are reading is a tragedy and the main character is a man who cannot make up his mind. Remember though, a tragedy is like a one-way trip on a road to doom," says the voice up front. "There's no turning back!"

"So, if the main guy is going to die anyway, why is he on that road?" a girl with greenish streaks in her hair and wearing a faded denim jacket asks. "Who cares?"

"Yeah, why waste our time?" demands a taller than tall boy at the back. "We already know what's going to happen."

"True, but as readers we are taken on his personal journey. What is interesting is the trip," replies the voice up front.

"Interesting to whom?" a girl with eyeglasses as wide as bottoms of two drinking glasses asks.

82

The room becomes a dark country road on a warm night and the voice up front is amazed by the utter quiet.

After several seconds, a boy sitting directly in front of the voice up front clears his throat and asks to speak.

"Go ahead," the voice up front responds and then nods at the boy.

"My cousin is like this Shakespeare character. But nobody killed him, he killed himself. Everyone knew it was only a matter of time."

"What happened?" the voice asks.

"He stopped drinking and rode his motorcycle to those alcoholic meetings. However, he never got well. In fact, one night, his wife was in the hospital having their third kid and he went to visit her. He first stopped at the liquor store and picked up a mickey of rye…just in case he felt the need to celebrate. In the waiting room, he could not stand it anymore and drank the whiskey. After his last gulp, he took out his Swiss Army knife and slashed both his wrists right there. Doctors could do nothing. I think his mind was made up, don't you? Did the Shakespeare character expect to die?"

"Not sure if the main character knew about the inevitable doom," the voice up front answers.

"Don't think my cousin knew much about Shakespeare. He quit school in Grade 8, but he knew there was no turning back."

"Someone once told me that Shakespeare got married at eighteen to a woman who was eight years older than him. They had three kids, like your cousin," the voice added.

"My cousin liked older women too. Did Billy Shakespeare keep to himself and drink lots? And I wonder how Shakespeare would do on a motorcycle?" the boy asks. "Bet he would do it with no helmet. And maybe… just maybe, he loved his bike so much that he would not have much time to write."

"Imagine," the voice up front replies. "Imagine that."

Politics

NEVER HAS THE VOICE UP FRONT HEARD THIS.

Suddenly, someone drops scissors on the floor and the entire room is a lung holding its breath.

"Do any of you discuss politics regularly at home?" the voice up front asks.

"Politics… it's like arguing about a favourite colour or sweater or snack," the voice up front hears from a boy in a purple T-shirt whose political IQ is sky-high. "Why bother?"

"But isn't it our duty to vote?" offers a short blue-haired girl in a yellow sweater who taps a pen on her right cheek.

"Duty? Listen, lots of voters simply do not vote for people who make them feel afraid. It eliminates lots of choices. Know what I mean?" says the boy in the purple T-shirt.

"What if you don't have a choice?" the voice up front asks.

"I protest. I protect. I take action."

"Protect? Protect who?"

"It could be my brother, my sister, my mother … anyone in my family who needs protecting."

"Give an example," says the voice. "And how is that connected to voting?"

"On the weekend, I sat up all night in the dark with a shotgun on my lap in a rocking-chair waiting for my father to come home," says the boy in the purple T-shirt in a matter-of-fact voice.

"Did I hear you correctly?" the voice up front asks.

"Yes, you did. And my family did not have to vote on it either. I just knew it was the only way to stop my father from scaring us anymore so I waited up for him. My own fear of him is gone. I threw it away in a faraway field."

"Did he come home?" someone exhales in a room so silent an October leaf could be heard scraping against an outside window.

"Nope," the boy in the purple T-shirt finally replies as he scans the room.

"Is your father that bad?" someone else asks.

"Yeah. And it might take some time to get him as he is probably still out there boozing and chasing women."

"What about your mom? What is she saying about all this?" the voice up front inquires wrinkling its forehead.

"Oh, she had her suitcase packed and sitting by the front door for weeks now. My father just laughs and kicks the suitcase whenever he goes out somewhere."

"All this started with politics and voting?" the voice up front offers cautiously.

"Kind of. But do you see my point?" the boy in the purple T-shirt asks. "It does not matter who is in power. What matters is if you feel afraid, then do not vote for that person. Eliminate them. That makes voting so easy!"

"Are you still waiting for your father?" asks the voice up front. "To eliminate him."

"Sure. Sooner or later, he will come home and I hope I am there when he arrives."

"So, what happens if he comes home and you are somewhere else?" a tall thin cautious boy inquires who sits closest to the door.

And someone drops another pair of scissors.

Never has the voice up front heard this.

Puff Evidence

Because of this puff evidence story, the voice up front becomes quiet with curiosity.

Three larger than large boys push their way to the back of a stuffed bus. One of them heaves open a window to the harsh winter wind. Then he lights up a cigarette being careful to aim the smoke outside. No one complains. Passengers just look out unopened windows and at the floor or ceiling. One man even inhales whatever leftover smoke he can, as if he cannot wait to light up one of his own.

Smoke evidence take shape in the air and a puff of smoke, the size of a dinner plate, settles on the first boy's right shoulder. The boy looks over to his right and tries to flick the puff away but the puff refuses to leave.

"What's that on your shoulder?" the second smoker asks.

"Yeah, what is that white shape? asks the third boy.

"Don't know," says the first boy. "Just ignore it."

Then each of the other two boys tries to get rid of the puff. They all blow. They fan. Textbooks are swung back and forth. Another window is opened. Nothing. Finally, the first boy stubs out his cigarette on the floor. By this time, the back of the bus is ice-cold and almost smoke-free except for the smell. Passengers disembark. One new passenger asks the driver: "Why is this bus so cold and stinks of smoke?"

The driver stops the bus and gets up from his seat. At the back, he notices the strong tobacco smell and the white puff on the boy's right shoulder.

"Smoking is not allowed on buses! And you must be the one who had a smoke," he says pointing to the first boy.

"How can you tell?"

"Look at that puff, that smoke still clinging to your right shoulder. That is real."

Do you see a cigarette in my hand?" the boy asks.

"No, but I see a butt on the floor by your feet."

"That could belong to anyone."

"I don't think so," the bus driver says. "Come with me."

"Where are we going?"

"To the front of the bus. I will report this."

The driver calls for a supervisor. "Have a seat right there."

Still perched on the boy's right shoulder is the puff.

"Proof is there for everyone to see," insists the driver.

"Why can't you admit that you were smoking on my bus?"

"Okay. Okay. It was me!"

As smooth as smoke set free, the puff slips down the boy's shoulder, curls through the air and vanishes through the open front door.

Both the boy and the bus driver become stone-faced at the truth of it all.

Might Have Been Better

WHO DESERVES TO BE IN THEIR OWN DRAMA?

After listening to a recording of Julius Caesar and following along in a textbook, one boy who has been known to have a detective-like mind suddenly laughs aloud.

"Okay, what's so funny?" asks the voice up front.

"It's the reader's funny British accent. Did all those Romans speak with an English accent? Isn't Rome in Italy?"

"Yes, but why didn't you laugh at the beginning when you first heard the accent?"

"I've been holding it in for the rest of the play and it hasn't been easy!"

"The recording was made in England using British actors," replies the voice up front.

"Why didn't they get Italian actors in Rome to do it? Weren't the characters in the play all Italian?"

"True, but... ."

Then one by one, the rest of the boys and girls chuckle unevenly. They crack their knuckles. Rub a pimple or two. Lick their teeth. Try out their British accents.

"With all this action, you guys should start a classroom parade for Julius Caesar," the voice up front suggests.

"Sure and I'll be Julius Caesar," said the detective boy with the first laugh.

Each person takes on a role and they cannot wait until they circle Caesar and pretend to stab him to death.

"See how easy it is to be fooled by people you think you know," the voice up front says.

"Yeah, just keep saying how great they are," says the detective boy who is known to be one of the smartest in the room. "Inevitably, they believe what they hear. Yesterday, after school, I saw a fight between two boys. The first guy looked at the second guy and told him that he was respected by so many, so why did he want to fight? Before the second boy could answer, the first guy asked: 'What's that in the sky?' When the second kid looked up, he got kicked hard, right in the crown jewels. The fight was over in seconds."

The voice up front then says: "At least the guy you saw only got kicked in the groin. Caesar got stabbed by people he knew. Those people even washed their hands and their swords in Caesar's blood!"

"In the scrap yesterday, all the guy did was pretend to wipe his hands clean and walk away," says the detective boy. No blood. Might have been better if Julius Caesar got kicked in the balls."

"Yeah. Sooner or later the pain goes away," says another boy looking down at his own crotch.

"So is this play a tragedy?" the voice up front asks. "Was Caesar headed to his unavoidable death?"

"Sure. He deceived himself. He never saw clearly what was going on around him. And by the way, he would not last an hour on the streets around here," a girl's voice offers from the back of the room.

"Maybe, but at least he might still be alive," says another girl with a face, like oak. "Beaten but alive."

"But for how long?" asks a tall boy dressed from head-to-toe in shades of brown.

"So what was Caesar's biggest problem?" asks the voice up front.

"Well, he is certainly not like us," replies a girl sitting by a window.

"Why?" the voice up front asks.

"Simple," replies the same girl. "He conned himself and believed in his own crap. That…is not us."

Rooftops

LIFE ON A ROOF HAS ITS OWN SCIENCE.

The boy, who is wider than he is taller, is ready on his stool in the biology lab and waits patiently for directions from the voice up front.

Then, staring out a window, he sees three rooftops with chimneys, TV antennas and TV satellite dishes. A tall angular woman on the closest rooftop hangs laundry on a grey clothes line. She explodes with waving when she sees the boy looking in her direction, but she may also be waving at a neighbour on another rooftop.

Meanwhile, the voice up front is still not ready, but tells everyone: "Be prepared to carefully observe."

The boy lets his thoughts roam from rooftop to rooftop and then back to the woman hanging up a pair of jeans. The hazy sky clears and a mid-morning sun suddenly shoots its rays between the legs of the jeans, and the boy on the stool smiles at the power of it all. Flinging her hands up to the sky, as if throwing sunlight back to the sun, the woman then begins sorting through more wet laundry in her basket. Right now, the boy may be unsure if she is singing to the wet clothes or talking to herself.

Over on the second rooftop, pigeons fly into a roost as a completely bald man with a full white beard applauds their return while sitting just below the roost. Then the bearded man lights up his pipe and the smoke has little chance to

form anything, not even a story about him because the wind
blows it all away quickly. Standing tall, he speaks to his birds
under a canopy of bright sky. The birds reply with their own
wing messages. Leaning even more towards the window and
almost slipping off the stool, the boy in the biology lab might
be imagining himself on that roof with the man, the birds
and their erratic dialogues.

On the third roof, so many TV antennas of various sizes
and lengths stand as clumps of bony scarecrows and this
roof belongs to them only. Some of their broken and twisted
arms almost cross over each other and are guarded by a black-
ened chimney. Their arms are a mystery, but they tell an open
story about their past.

The boy on the lab stool listens to the tale coming from
the black tar pages of the roof. In the story he is shown how
to stand still when watching and listening to life on a roof.
Two of the antennas seem to want to hold hands, but are
hesitant because of several TV satellite dishes perched on
one side of the roof eyeing their every move. Because the
satellite dishes now do most of the work, the TV antennas
are nothing more than aluminum ribs taking up space.

What looks like a black and white striped cat, runs along
the tin edge of the second roof where the pigeons are. It
stops quickly to have a second and third look at the pigeon
roost. The man with the white beard flings a few roof pebbles at the cat and the animal is swallowed up by sunlight.

Right then the voice up front calls for everyone's attention. "Take a look at the slide under each of your micro-
scopes. Write down exactly what you see."

"Can I imagine something too?" the boy asks.

"Of course, but start with what's in front of you."

"Sure."

"Is there anything else?"

"I'll let you know," replies the boy.

Life on a roof has its own science.

Fire and Fruit

NO ONE KNEW THE BOY WOULD SHARE THIS TRUTH. NO ONE.

"Do you know anyone who's been jailed, like the story we're reading?" the voice up front asks.

One boy, with a scar on his chin that curls to the left below his bottom lip, looks at another boy sitting next to him who smiles and nods. Heads turn and look at one another and the room becomes a ripple of faces moving like a wave that lost its direction. Most of them have heard about the boy with the scar. They know about his prison father, the rage. The boy with the scar carries that knowledge as a hidden badge and hesitates to share it with the voice up front. Some of the others know that the boy's father is also a retired fireman who had taken great pride in his job. And the boy's biological mother is the fireman's second wife, the second of his four marriages.

"Tell the voice up front about your father," a girl in an orange blouse whispers behind the boy.

"Yeah, speak up. Talk about your dad," implores a second girl dressed from head to toe in green who could pose on the front of a bag of frozen peas.

"Please," hisses the boy. "Not now."

"Speak up about what?" the voice up front asks looking straight at the boy.

The boy with the scar looks to his left, his right and then takes a quick peek behind him.

"Nothing," he replies, his eyes glued to the voice up front. "Nothing at all."

"About prisons," the voice continues sweeping its eyes over the room. "Should everyone who has broken the law go to prison?"

"You break the law, you pay!" a voice from the back of the room proclaims.

"My father doesn't talk to me very much," the boy with the scar suddenly blurts out. "He says I am too much like him."

"How does that fit in with our discussion about prisons?" asks the voice up front.

"I never go visit my father in prison anymore because he says I am just like him and that I am in my own jail. He was a fireman and he was good at it. But his anger is worse than any fire. If you cannot think like he does, he blows up. It is the burning inside... he cannot put it out."

The room becomes so quiet a creaking chair sounds like an exclamation mark.

"Do you want to share why your father is in jail or...?" asks the voice up front.

"Ah, it does not matter anymore. My father is in the slammer for hitting his fourth wife with a hammer. He broke both of her wrists when she tried to protect herself. Anyhow, he does not drink anymore and I hear he tells everyone in prison that life is good."

"Do you think that is true?" the voice up front inquires ever so measuredly.

"My stepmom tried to talk to him last week about support payments. Was not a good idea. I mean he is in jail so what is he supposed to do for cash? Then he told her that the inmates do not trust him; they cannot see how his life is good!"

Outside the wind threatens to blow its way into the room so it too can hear what the boy will say. The voice up front shuts the last open window and exhales at the glass.

"Maybe, your father is comparing his life before prison and now," the voice up front offers.

"Isn't that like comparing apples and oranges? Didn't you tell us about that some time ago when we discussed another story? Know something? My father hates fruit. He says it goes straight through him."

No one knew the boy would share this truth. No one.

Hurricane Breathing

How REAL IS THIS TALK, THIS TRYING TO BREATHE IN A HURRICANE?

"A sociologist... does anyone know what a sociologist does for a living?" the voice up front asks.

"Isn't that someone who orders rainbow-coloured paint for the walls to make the place look good?" asks a boy with spiked blond hair sitting by the window. The boy's question is a spotless response and the room becomes a place where the inhaling is new.

"And don't they want to install new carpets, big windows and central stairways so we can meet more people and be happier?"

"Maybe," answers the voice up front.

"That is not like a social worker. Nope. I know what a social worker does," offers a small and incredibly thin girl whose xylophone bones burst from her skin.

"All of them do something social... social this and... social that. Does that mean they are all friendly?" someone else asks, the question like a cloud approaching the sun.

"Maybe," the small thin girl answers in a hesitant voice. "Maybe."

"You sound like you might know something about social workers," the voice up front says to the slender girl.

"Maybe, I should not share this but...my social worker never says a word about paint, carpets, windows or stairways.

She just wants me to be at peace. When I was two, my parents took off to a party and left me strapped in my highchair for two straight days. Apparently, I cried and cried and nobody came. I sat in my own pee and poo for two full days. Finally, a neighbour heard my howling and called Social Services. When the social worker found me, the kitchen was a toilet. And I had cried myself dry."

"But what makes you remember all that? Should you be talking with our counsellor" asks the voice up front sounding as gentle as tissue paper.

"No. Right here is fine. How can I ever forget! She keeps in touch. Whenever I enter a washroom today, no matter how clean it looks, the smell makes me puke. The social worker warned me that smell can be a big memory trigger."

"Too bad those sociologists couldn't remember to add a nice smell to all that coloured paint," a boy offers whose face is splashed with a maze of freckles. "There are some nice smells, like chocolate or popcorn or meat cooking in a frying pan. Those smells are like friends. Enemies do not help us make more friends."

"Who leaves a toddler alone for two days," the small, thin girl almost shouts.

The room becomes so quiet that the shuffling of shoes on the floor is louder than ever imagined.

"So what happened to your parents afterwards?" the voice up front asks.

"Never saw them again. I was immediately placed in a foster home."

"Were you happy?"

"Well, there was no rainbow paint on the walls. The carpets were old and smelly. Windows were mostly covered. And there were no stairs anywhere, except for those going down to a dark basement where I never went. I did not meet many new people. I stopped pretending to be happy because I learned long ago how to breathe in a hurricane."

The chalkboard creaks. The clock ticks hammer-like. And the blaring sun demands a response.

How real is this talk, this trying to breathe in a hurricane?

Certain Books

Harold's solitude comes from reading certain books.

The seventeen-year-old in the long-sleeved, cloud-white shirt moves carefully by the bookshelves. He floats through his own sky and almost holds his breath, as if each book is a shrine. Anytime soon it will happen. The librarian knows. She never has to tell Harold. She hesitates to say that time is up. Once Harold finds what he wants, he... vanishes.

Today is no different. Harold disappears into the stacks. Everyone else settles at tables, returns books or browses. Some need to be quieted. Others are directed to specific sections. Life in the library is slow, easy and pouring into the room at a steady pace is the afternoon sun.

When the library period ends, Harold is nowhere to be found.

"Let's look for him," says the voice up front. "Spread out."

Some boys head straight for the magazine section.

"Not here," someone says.

A second group of two girls and one boy move over to the shelves and begin the search. They look high. They look low. They look behind. No Harold.

Some return from the hallway, the room at the back of the library and the washrooms and shrug.

"Maybe Harold took off home," a girl holding three library books says.

"Could be," says the voice up front. "Okay everyone, back to the room."

As they leave, one girl asks: "But what about Harold?"

When they return, there sitting on top of Harold's desk, is a murder mystery book. "He's got to be somewhere," the voice up front says.

Everyone slides into their desks and looks back at Harold's open book. The voice up front moves towards Harold's desk, picks up the murder mystery book and then shakes it. Nothing.

"Where are you, Harold?" the voice up front asks.

The next morning Harold shows up for class and the voice up front asks again: "Where have you been , Harold?"

"Thinking like a murderer," Harold replies. "Outside of school."

Then the voice up front hands Harold his book.

"Did the story take you somewhere?"

"Sure and I didn't want to come back," says Harold.

"We looked all over the library for you. What happened?"

"Well...I left school after reading the first few pages of my book and went hunting for the murderer in my book. First time I have done that. I had to find out on my own."

"How do you do it, Harold? How do you fall into a story like that?"

"Well, I do not sign out a book from the library. The book signs me out. My parents and teachers have tried to point me to other books. Nothing worked. Murder mysteries are all I read now. I am hooked.

"But why don't you simply read the rest of your book to find out?" the voice up front asks.

"Too easy," Harold replies.

Harold's solitude comes from reading certain books.

Third Floor Red

SINCE THE DOCTOR TOLD HIM THAT HE SHOULD NOT GIVE anymore, my father has never felt better.

"Check this out," the girl in the toe-length, red, red Valentine's Day skirt almost shouts down the hall.

The girl in the long red skirt prances from one doorway to the next showing off the colour red at the doorway of each room. When she arrives at the room belonging to the voice up front, the girl is invited inside.

"Sure, come on in", the voice up front says. "Show us your red."

"Like what you see?" the girl asks with her head held high.

People clap, cheer and thump on their desks.

"You seem to be redder than red today," the voice up front says.

"But it's not that dark blood red, like so many Valentine cards," the girl replies. "That deep red...it makes me think of why my father stopped donating blood a couple of years ago."

"And what's the connection between blood and Valentine's Day?" asks the voice up front.

"Well, his blood type is rare: AB, Rh positive. And they called so often for him to donate. One Valentine's Day, he was called at work and asked if he would show up at the hospital operating room within the hour. Imagine… they needed my father's blood type right away."

"Did he go?"

"Yeah, but his boss was not too pleased. Someone had to fill in for my dad. But he reminded his boss that Valentine's Day is a day of love."

"So, what happened?"

"He drove like a fanatic filled with love to the hospital and barely had time to take off his coat. They put him on a gurney and wheeled him into the O.R."

"Must have been scary."

"Sure was. Doctors were performing open-heart surgery on a truck driver who was just a few years older than my father. My dad forgot to eat his lunch which was a bad move so they gave him a few of those giant chocolate chip cookies and orange juice. But it was a bit late. He fainted as the nurse was getting everything ready. They let him rest for a while and when he woke up, he felt kind of weak and wanted to go home. They gave him more cookies and juice."

"Did he leave after that?" the voice up front asks.

"Nope, not after he was reminded that his blood would save the trucker's life, so they tried the IV in my father's arm again. He was fine right up until they took the last of the blood from him. Then he fainted once more. So they left him alone next to the trucker."

"Oh. Was your dad okay after that?"

"Not really. When he woke up, they moved him outside the O.R. where he rested some more."

"How did he get back home?" asks the voice up front.

"My mother took a taxi from her work to the hospital and then drove them both home in our car. I really do not mean this to be a bad joke but on every Valentine's Day since then, my father wears dark sunglasses to avoid the colour red… just in case."

Since the doctor told him that he should not give any-more, my father has never felt better.

Hallway Presence

"I WANT THIS TO SEEM ACCIDENTAL SO CAN YOU PRETEND TO look the other way?" the girl whispers loudly over her shoulder as she inches towards the open doorway.

The voice up front stands near the doorway watching older bodies float by until a long tall glass of water of a boy stops and peeks into the room.

"Can you tell me the name of that chocolate-eyed girl sitting near the window?" he politely asks the voice up front.

"Go and ask her yourself," the voice replies. "But make it quick as we are starting class soon."

The boy steps into the room while the voice up front smiles and slowly shakes its head. Before long the tall boy and the girl are grinning madly, the girl in particular, her head bursting with long, thick, black hair, like random punctuation marks.

"Thanks," the boy says to the voice up front as he exits the room.

About an hour later, the long, tall boy is back and peeking into the voice up front's window which is noticed by the voice up front and the dark-eyed girl. He remains at the window and only moves away when the voice up front walks towards the door, smiles and turns back.

Meanwhile the girl fidgets at her desk and then studies the clock on the wall, as if nudging the hour hand to move faster.

Just before lunch, the boy's face again appears at the window. This time he gives a quick wave towards the girl and then vanishes. The voice up front does not notice, but the girl certainly does. She crosses her legs one way and then the other. Then she folds her arms over her heart and shifts back and forth in her seat.

At lunch, the girl searches everywhere for the boy and he looks for her too, but they do not meet. All their searching allows no time for lunch.

In the afternoon, the girl is back in the room with the voice up front. Within seconds after the door is closed, the tall boy appears again at the window in the top half of the door. This time he stares straight at the girl and ignores all the faces looking back at him. When the girl notices everyone looking at the door, she throws up her hands as if to ask: "where were you at lunchtime?" The boy also flings his hands upward and his eyes plead for one more chance. When the voice up front finally turns to face everyone after writing on the chalkboard, it too notices all eyes facing the door. Almost immediately, the boy's face disappears.

At the end of the day, the dark-eyed girl stays after everyone leaves to ask the voice up front a question. The room's door is wide open to the completion of another day.

"Do you remember that boy who came into the room to talk to me this morning?" she asks the voice up front.

"I sure do," replies the voice up front. "And he might be waiting for you outside in the hallway. See that shadow? It could be him."

"What if it's not him?"

"But what if it is? I mean... who really knows with shadows?"

"Okay, but I want this to seem accidental...even to you, so can you pretend to look the other way?" the girl whispers loudly over her shoulder as she inches towards the open doorway.

Never Been Run Over

"Doesn't matter," says the voice up front. "I need some fresh air."

The voice up front is being chauffeured by another voice up front and several boys stand in front of the crawling vehicle. As the car moves, so do the boys. They wave and stand their ground until the car can barely advance. Then they all become like Clint Eastwood, as if they had never been run over before. With gritted teeth, the boys dig their hands into their hips and stop the car right there. The voice up front rolls down a window and jokes: "Okay, we give up! What's happening? When's your next movie?"

"Just try to get by," a few boys shout.

"Okay," says the driver. "Why not."

So, the driver slips it into REVERSE and backs up quite a distance to the fence. Shocked, the boys are frozen in their shoes.

"You're not thinking of... ," the voice up front says to the driver.

"Watch me," says the driver who then revs his motor and spins his rear wheels.

With that, most of the boys scatter for their lives except for two who stand tall at the exit. There are no more "just try" words but the driver and the voice up front know. Then the driver shifts his car into DRIVE, keeps his foot on the brake pedal and honks his horn over and over. Gunning the engine even more, he lets go of the brake and speeds straight towards the two boys. Just before the vehicle is about to run the boys over, the two boys leap to the side and the vehicle stops exactly where the boys stood beforehand.

"You really were going to run us over," shouts one of the two boys.

"You're crazy!" the second boy screams. "Insane!"

"Maybe," the driver yells out his window. "Maybe."

As they drive off, the voice up front asks: "What were you thinking?"

"Did you want to be taken hostage by those guys?" the driver asks.

"Hostage… what are you talking about?"

"Those boys were trying to intimidate us!"

"No, they were just being silly."

"You're telling me that you didn't feel threatened when they blocked the exit?"

"Nope, they would have soon left if we just smiled and ignored them."

"I can't believe that's how you saw it," the driver mutters.

"Perception is a small part of reality," the voice up front reminds the driver. "And the reality is that those guys were just fooling around."

"Well, you saw it that way but it wouldn't be the real Clint Eastwood's reality. Didn't you hear what those boys said?"

"Yes, I did," I say.

"Well?"

"Well, kids watch movies and they sometimes imitate what they see."

"Then I guess you and I see the world differently," says the driver.

"Could be. Why don't you drop me off here?"

"But we haven't arrived at where we're going."

"Doesn't matter," says the voice up front. "I need some fresh air."

Sleep Walkers and The Secretary

AT THE MAIN OFFICE, A SINGLE FILE OF SLEEP WALKERS WAITS FOR late slips in an in-between world.

The secretary works in slow motion today filling out forever slips as the line of bodies grows longer. She looks and sounds like she has cobwebs in her brain. Her mouth is desert-dry because she keeps smacking her lips. Red lines map the whites of her eyes. Smelling as if she spent the night in a whiskey bottle, any paper shuffling for her might sound like an oncoming freight train. Each late person builds her resentment for being here and her grumbling increases with each new late slip, her face gradually balling into fists

Finally one boy in line says: "You don't look so good. "

"Just mind your own business!" she replies. "Here's your late slip."

Another girl pinches her own nose while facing the secretary.

"You have a nose problem, young lady?" the secretary asks.

"Sort of," the girl answers.

"Well, what is it?"

"My mother drinks and talks to her murder-mystery books at night. You smell like her."

"I don't read murder-mystery books."

"So what do you read then?"

"Me read? I make phone calls to my family and friends and tell them what I think of them."

"My mother does that too sometimes, usually late at night."

"No matter. Here is your late slip."

The next one in line is a boy who might look and feel like the secretary. Not a word is exchanged.

"You look like I feel. Better get going. Take your slip," the secretary says.

Next is a tall, blonde girl, her hair springing up like white knitting needles, looks as if she just fell out of bed.

"And what's your excuse?" the secretary asks.

"Flipping burgers last night," the girl replies. "I'm beat."

"Well, take this late slip. Now get going."

Another boy, who is as thin as a fishing rod, runs his hand over his brush-cut head and gives his name.

"And why are YOU late?" the secretary asks.

"It's my father," he answers. "He came home drunk with another woman last night and woke us all up. Imagine, he asked my mother if she had any spare clothes for this other woman."

"What?"

"My mom was already yelling. Right away she ran into the kitchen and grabbed a butcher's knife. Then she threatened my father and the other woman. The police showed up. What a mess!"

"But why oh why... are you even here today?" asks the secretary, her head now throbbing and threatening to burst.

"Nowhere else to go," the boy replies.

At the main office, a single file of sleep walkers waits for late slips in an in-between world.

Must Be Still Inside

"THE SMELLS...THE SOUNDS... WILL NOT GO AWAY," THE BOY says.

Within minutes, the building empties because of a fire drill with the oldest boys and girls emerging last. Roll call is taken and the voice up front notices that someone is missing.

"I know he is here today," the voice up front says aloud to no one near the steps to the main entrance. "Maybe he is still inside."

Later, after everyone heads back inside, the voice up front discovers the boy still at his desk with his head buried in his arms. The others leave for lunch.

"What happened to you?" the voice asks.

"I tried to follow everyone outside, but couldn't move."

"Why? What happened?"

"It's my mom. In the small town we moved from, she forgot to take her medication one day and was burnt to death inside our house during a snowstorm."

"So what does that have to do with your staying inside during our fire drill today?"

"It happened a year ago when I was at school in that town. I wanted to try and feel how she died without the medication, but there was no real fire here."

"You may have put your own life at risk."

"No, I would have gotten out in time... I think."

"What happened to your mother?"

"Someone from the town fire department said that they found her holding onto her purse near the wood stove, as if maybe she were trying to protect her purse from the flames."

"Too bad she forgot her medication at the time," the voice up front says.

"Yeah, well she usually always took her meds. Kept them in her purse mostly. Anytime some new medication was brought home, my ma would fondle the bottle, like it was a sacred object."

The voice up front imagines the boy's mother caressing her purse and not realizing that she was surrounded by flames. The carpet around her burns brightly, the flames creating an alphabet of wonder for the mother's eyes. The mother reads the story of her life in hues of orange, red, yellow and blue. Because she feels no pain or too much pain, she laughs loudly at the sounds of the fire engines arriving and the smoke... the endless smoke.

"Only the carpet is on fire. It will burn itself out in no time," the mother says. "No danger. My insides feel like my outsides... hot... hotter. Gotta get this purse somewhere safe. I am cold. I am hot. I am cold. I am hot. Time to go to sleep now. No one will know. No one will know. Where the hell are my meds...where are they?"

"Are you hungry?" asks the voice up front.

"Starving," answers the boy.

"Me too. Time for lunch."

"But my mother's fire... I can still hear the crackling."

"Feels like it's still burning... somewhere," says the voice up front. "But not here."

"The smells... the sounds... will not go away," the boy says.

Between Frustration and Boredom

"WAIT. WHAT IF WILLY LOMAN CHANGED?" ASKS A TINY GIRL turning her head, her face cringing.

Row upon row of heads suddenly all look at each other with an odd mix of calmness and then... urgency.

"For now, let us imagine that I am Willy. My life is so chaotic and I never know it."

"Okay. Willy...Willy, where are you right now?" a boy asks between measured breaths.

"Look up," says the voice up front. "I'm here, right here."

"And what are you selling today?" inquires a girl sitting near the front.

"Yeah, we all know you pretend to be a salesman and have two sons, one of whom says you simply had the wrong dream," another girl says.

Maybe wrong dreams are born between frustration and boredom. They know guys like Willy Loman.

"I will make it. You will see. I...am Willy Loman!" shouts the voice up front.

"How can anyone get excited about you, Willy?" someone demands. "I mean you don't even dream properly when you're awake!"

"And didn't one of your sons catch you in a hotel room with another woman?" another asks. "You sure know how to lie. And always borrowing money from a neighbour.

We know, Willy. We know. You pretend that you earned it by selling something. That is crap!"

"How can my dream be wrong?" the voice up front implores. "How can any dream be wrong?"

"You're a loser, Willy," someone shouts. "You are gone and not coming back!"

"Then how do you make a wrong dream right?" asks the voice up front. "Come on, tell me. Pretend. Imagine."

"Know something? You need to work on your brain, Willy… where dreams start. Begin by being straight with yourself and your family. Your wife will not find out about that other woman; yet, she probably already knows. Then get a real job, Willy. Forget this sales garbage, will ya," a huge red-haired boy suggests from the back of the room.

"You have all the answers," the voice up front says.

"No, I just know that my own father lives in a fairy-tale world too. He is a liar… always talking about his next big deal which never ever comes, like Willy Loman does. Big shot. My father really believes he is a wheeler and dealer. My mom works two jobs just to pay the bills. My big brother works full-time loading trucks. I work part-time at a fast-food joint, which is not such a bad thing, except that we have to give most of our pay to my mother who doesn't want us to turn out like our father."

"Did your father have the wrong dream too, like Willy Loman in our play?" the voice up front asks.

"Yeah, but I think he may have planned it that way."

"How can anyone plan a wrong dream? How?"

"Ask my father. He knows about pretending," the red-haired boy replies.

"Well…why don't we give Willy Loman a break for now?"

"Good idea," says the red-haired boy. "He is a waste of time. He will never change. Also, he is a character in a play. Not a real father."

"Maybe," says the voice up front. "Sometimes, people and their dreams can surprise us."

Raindrop Codes

"CAN'T YOU SEE? LOOK HARD," THE VOICE UP FRONT SAYS TO everyone.

One by one, all ears switch to listen to the sedative tap-tapping of a late November rain. Then the voice up front stands by one of the windows finger-counting the drops dripping and streaking down the glass. Slowly, every person in the room gets up and moves towards the windows. Creating its own code on the glass, the raindrops become letters, then words, then stories. People take turns reading their glass stories to each other. Every narrative becomes new with each reader. Because it seems so easy to read each one, the voice up front decides to have students tell what they see and perhaps act out the plot.

The first window shows a young girl's tears after she discovers that her older brother has been taking drugs. She knows what her brother is doing but feels helpless. After begging him to stop on numerous occasions, the girl tries hiding his stash, but he catches her doing it and smacks her across the face. Her tears criss-cross on her reddened cheeks and trickle down her neck where they pool just above her ribcage. Suddenly realizing what he has done, the brother runs from the room, with a tail of regret following him."

"Did he ever stop taking drugs?" the voice up front inquires.

"Probably," replies a girl whose eyes are made to be inquisitive. "He's now in a treatment centre."

The second story has two grandparents laughing so hard at their secret and then their hands cover each other's faces, like tiny flocks of birds. The more one of them tries to speak, the harder they laugh. Eyes swell and water up so much that they float and bob in their sockets and barely hang on because of their shaking heads. The grandparents then cough and choke away the rest of their laughter until they both collapse next to each other on a sofa. The grandpa makes a lame joke about sex and how he is being too hard on grandma. And the grandma replies he should be stiffer more often. Their sighs are so loud because they have laughed themselves dry.

"What's so funny with that older couple?" asks the voice up front.

"They're still in love", answers a tall girl with dark eyes and whose voice pretends to be old. "Can't you see? Cannot keep their hands off each other!"

The third window has a man watching a movie about the first black player to play major league baseball. The boy's dead father just lived and breathed baseball. As the film continues, the boy keeps wiping the tears from his eyes because he remembers his dad telling him about the heart of the story on the screen. It is impossible to turn off his father's voice. So many tears take over the boy's face that he thinks he watches the movie underwater.

"How does the film end?" asks the voice up front.

"Everyone... and I mean everyone in the audience stands up and claps. Unbelievable!" says the boy.

"And what about the guy underwater...you?"

"Well... he was probably the first one to walk off that movie set to get some fresh air," says another boy who needs his hands to talk.

"Can't you see? Look hard," the voice up front says to everyone.

The Wasting

"I CAN TELL."

In the room, the voice up front lets everyone continue talking about the weekend hockey game because several people let the voice know that they are "being logical and demonstrating insight into human behaviour." Their words. One armchair critic after another emphasizes each point to make sure the discussing continues.

Meanwhile, the voice up front looks at its watch, throws up its hands, exhales slowly and listens. All the talking is worth more than what the voice had planned. The recall of game details is more than accurate. The thinking between the lines is brilliant. Critical thoughts make the hockey game sound like a game of chess. This is a victory for everyone who wins the game of reasoning and precision. This is a loss for anyone who thinks that talking is always a waste of time.

Right then, the throwing away of time brings the voice up front faraway to the Rocky Mountains where the voice stands before a cool, blue-green lake named after a woman called Princess Louise Caroline Alberta, the fourth daughter of Queen Victoria. If only the princess knew how the lake helped the voice up front realize the value of depleted minutes. Then the voice up front sees himself sitting on a long, pale log which is mostly pointing out to the middle of Lake Louise. Boulders piled up behind the log on dry land are the knuckles of a giant hand. The hand might belong to the voice up front's father. The father loved to imagine and routinely encouraged the voice up front to do the same.

"Remember, it must take your breath away, Son," the father says.

"I see mountain peaks wearing glacial sweaters. I see awestruck people paddling canoes on blue-green glass. I see, what might be, two lovers horseback riding, perhaps for the first time, and both horses feel their passion."

"Good," replies the father. "Thinking like that will keep you safe when you least expect it."

Suddenly the voice up front hears it. The silence in the room is deafening. The wasting in the room is over. Everyone watches the voice up front staring off into nowhere.

After the bell rings, a girl dressed in red and white asks the voice: "You look like you stopped breathing there for a while. What happened? We all finished talking about the hockey game some time ago."

"Well…I've been standing in front of Lake Louise.

"Lake Louise? That is a long way from here."

"My father had a hand in all of it."

"What do you mean?"

"My father's always with me."

"Okay, but what did you plan for us?"

"It can wait until tomorrow."

"Will your father be here?"

"Sure. In spirit. He taught me how to give my breath away," replies the voice up front.

"I know," says the girl dressed in red and white. "I can tell."

For God's Sake

"I CAN BREATHE BETTER ALREADY," THE BOY SAYS.

Looking over the room, the voice up front recalls a group Germans playing chess on a Costa del Sol beach by the Mediterranean Sea. He remembers them vividly from a summer trip to Spain. The Germans did not laugh very much but when they did, their howling blew through the sunlight and exploded over the sea, like breakers breaking. Between chess moves, each pair of players kept gesturing toward the sky, the water and to bathers around them, as if they were trying to prove the existence of something and the chess game itself was simply an excuse to find this proof.

"Does God exist?" the voice up front asks after freeing itself of its Spanish memory.

Everyone is already paired up and ready to debate. An angling boy in a pink shirt raises both of his hands and says: "conscience and submission."

"What does conscience and then submission have to do with whether God exists or not?" asks his partner, a stern-looking girl who keeps pushing her eyeglasses up her nose. "I have enough guilt for a lifetime. And I heard that God will punish me, so He must exist, right?"

"Yeah, God's right there... in my notes," adds a lone sentinel rocking back and forth in his chair and who is barely participating because of his bad head cold.

"No, there is no God. But if there ever was a real God, he or she would be loving. Only a loving God can exist. That punishing God is made by people who go to church," says a short, black-haired girl who is dressed from head-to-toe in white and who is a top achiever in everything. "And remember, all churches are institutions and institutions are made up of people and people are fallible…they screw up."

"Great discussion!" replies the voice up front. And for those of you who do believe, where would God be right now?"

Another boy sitting by a window and known for his probing comments exclaims: "He might be a handful of sun" and the boy allows his face to be warmed by insistent fingers of sunlight.

Someone else nibbling on the top of an inanimate ball-point pen stops and says: "God's got me in His arms right now… according to my mom, but… my mother is sometimes full of nonsense. Her arms don't work like God's."

"Then where is God?" the voice up front asks. "And what do you think God would look like?"

"The usual. You know…some tall, skinny guy with blue eyes, long brown hair, booming voice, a beard, and dressed in an enormous white cloud," someone else replies.

"No, I think God would be dressed in black, including his hood, because He likes to punish and wants us to find him," another voice states matter-of-factly.

"How can you say that? God is in all of us. He does not need to look like anything or anyone." a girl with too much body weight replies squirming in her chair. "What's the matter with you all anyway?"

"I don't see a God in you," proclaims another voice. "Can you see God in me?"

"Nope," answers someone else.

"Well… I see God in me," the girl says.

"Hold on everyone, God's right here," the lone boy with the bad head cold suddenly interrupts as he trumpets out the waddings of his nose into a tissue and examines closely the results of his efforts, as if God lay scattered on the softness of his world.

"I can breathe better already."

Second Side

"WELL, THAT'S HOW I SEE YOUR FUTURE."

Clusters of heads dip to the left and to the right, as if saying: "let me see your answers." An algebraic hum fills this room of recitation. A boy, trying to grow a beard, beams his sight upward to a hocus-pocus ceiling that absorbs the scattered snickering. And then a potbellied boy blows a perfect pink bubble of gum.

"Ah, the answers... who has them and who hasn't?" asks the voice up front.

"I don't," responds an older boy sitting alone by the chalkboard, who is already losing his hair and who isn't the least concerned about numbers. "And it doesn't matter."

"Why is that?" the voice up front inquires as he approaches the older boy.

"Later," he says waving at nothing.

"Okay," replies the voice up front.

After the room empties, the boy-man approaches the voice up front with caution.

"I...I quit school a few years ago and then came back this year."

"What made you return?"

"It was the glass. I needed to be on the other side of the glass."

"What do you mean?"

120

"While living on the streets, I walked by houses and apartment buildings and took quick looks through the windows. I saw people sitting around tables and eating. Some were talking with each other. Others watched TV. Still others teased each other and laughed big beautiful laughter. One night I even saw a man crying and his wife had her hand on his shoulder trying to make him feel better; first time I ever saw a man cry. Another night I saw a woman hanging her coat in a closet. Imagine that…a closet. Later, I saw a father sitting close to his young son on a sofa and reading a book to him; I thought I was watching a TV commercial or one of those old family shows from the 1950's or early 1960's that sometimes come on TV. Everything … everything looked better on the other side of the glass and I wanted to be there."

"But how come numbers don't mean that much to you?" the voice up front asks.

"It really doesn't matter about the number of windows I looked into, it was all the same. I was on the wrong side of the glass."

"So you came back here to learn how to get on the second side of the glass?"

"Yes, I love that number 'second'. I need that answer. And I am learning that there are other numbers."

"Okay then," the voice up front says. "Come with me."

"Where are we going?"

"To the window."

"Why?"

"You'll see."

At the window, the sky is painted in a hopeful clarity of white on powder blue and the voice up front asks: "Now tell me, do you see an end to that big sky out there?"

"Nope," says the mature student.

"Well, that's how I see your future."

Stay Little

"I WAS RAISED TO STAY LITTLE," THE SHORT BLONDE GIRL whispers, her chin almost touching her chest.

"Really?" the voice up front asks.

"It's my father. He's a lawyer and he was born with a mouthful of trouble which is his curse. He himself has been little all his life. He will never be bigger. When I hear him talk, I want to shrink. He needs to be right all the time. Do all short lawyers behave like that? Last night I dreamt that I sent only his mouth to a faraway island."

"What happened?"

"He had been out drinking again. After he left the bar, he had a speeding contest with two other drivers on the main highway. One driver slammed into a guardrail and was killed while the other driver ended up in a ditch and later the hospital."

"And your father?"

"Nothing. Not a scratch. Told us he won the race but he always says that."

"What about the police?" asks the voice up front.

"That's when it got complicated."

"How?"

"In my father's opinion, the police officer who arrested him was legally wrong. My father said the cop was a woman who was at least twenty pounds overweight.

"Because of all that doughnut dust on your chest, I am unable to see your badge number," he said to her.

"Then what happened?"

"The cop laughed while slapping the handcuffs on him and the more he mentioned the doughnut dust, the tighter she made the cuffs."

"Was he jailed?"

"Yes. Later, he appeared in court and represented himself. The judge asked him if he enjoyed having a fool to represent himself."

"Did he lose his driver's license?"

"Got it suspended."

"So how's he getting to work?"

"Takes the bus and walks the rest of the way. My mother refuses to drive him and says the exercise will do him good," says the girl.

"But what made you so late again today?" asks the voice up front.

On the wall above the door, the ticking clock reminds them both that missed minutes can never be retrieved today or any other day.

"When he wakes up every morning, my father makes us all feel tiny. He demands that we listen to his imagined suffering. My mother often tells him to get off his cross because we need the wood. This morning was especially horrible," says the girl. "My mother pushed him over the top when she told him that resentment is like swallowing poison to get even with someone."

"How did your father respond to that?"

"He lost his mouth. Really! I think he swallowed it, left, and slammed the door, just like a little kid I once knew," she says. "But like I said, I was raised to stay little."

Skins

No, THIS IS NOT A CARTOON.

There in the first seat by the window sits a boy whose ears are so prominent that it looks as if his nose and mouth have almost vanished from his face. Or perhaps his face no longer has any use for a nose or mouth. Each of the boy's huge blue eyes has a small dark, shiny pupil.... perfect places to hide secrets. And his eyebrows, thick and black, arch upwards and, if removed from his face, could be used as miniature boomerangs. The part in the boy's perfectly-combed hair has grown wider over time perhaps because intensive brushing and combing or maybe too much worrying. This boy's face is frozen in something.

Now, what happened to the boy's nose and mouth? Were they both so overwhelmed by the power of what his ears discovered that they simply shrunk in size? Or maybe the boy's mouth has nothing more to say.

Then the voice up front privately finds out what happened.

Recently the boy had heard in detail about his great-grandfather in France who had sent thousands of Jewish men, women and children, his own people, to the Nazi ovens. Each of these victims were French Jews. The boy had always admired his ancestors and had heard how much of an outstanding community leader his great-grandfather had been.

124

However, one afternoon, he discovered a box of letters in the basement to confirm what he heard. The letters were written by his great-grandfather to a Nazi commander in Paris during the German occupation of France. He denounced all Jews and apologized for their existence. To give the letters more immediacy, more power, the great-grandfather wrote each letter as if he were sitting next to the Nazi commander.

The boy's eyes, and particularly his ears, had been frozen open in shock and shame. How could his great-grandpa commit such acts? Perhaps because of guilt and shame, the boy's mouth nearly vanished as he certainly did not want to talk about it. His nose too had almost disappeared because he wanted to forget the ovens.

"Is there anything I can do to help?" asks the voice up front.

The boy grabs a piece of chalk and writes the following question in bold letters on the chalkboard: "HOW DO YOU WEAR A JEWISH SKIN?"

Nothing. Not a single response from anyone.

"Again, how does one wear a Jewish skin?" the voice up front asks everyone.

"Maybe, we just can't wear that kind of skin," a girl with chestnut curly hair springing from her head finally replies. "Quite honestly, I do not know how to wear a French skin or Portuguese skin or Polish skin or Greek skin or even an English skin for that matter. How do you wear a skin that belongs to someone else? I am Italian. I wear Italian skin. I know what that means. I cannot expect you to wear Italian skin like me. Right?"

Then all eyes are on the boy with the large ears. As they watch, his nose gradually re-appears, like magic, and then his mouth.

"But I can never think like my great-grandfather," the boy says. "Even though we wore the same skin."

No, this is not a cartoon.

From A Few Doors Down

CAREFULLY PLANNED AND THEN QUIET AT JUST THE RIGHT TIMES, the voice from a few doors down leads a busy life raising both honey bees and teenagers at home. This voice may also have intentions bigger than its doorway. And its laughter comes from a tap that turns on and off with the drop of its random smile.

Whenever that distressed woman, the one that people avoid here, fills its open doorway, the voice from a few doors down laughs its measured laugh.

Is there a reason for this measured response to a disturbed woman? Is it because the voice from a few doors down wants to be liked by those who seem troubled?

Could the bees have something to do with it? Maybe, the voice from a few doors down is really a worker bee doing its own dance movements to let other bees know where the best food is found, usually a large cluster of flowers. Yes, the voice even grows bushes of imaginary flowers in its doorway. That uneasy woman, who breathes the idea that hostility is a smokescreen for fear, goes there to smell that safe, sweet fragrance. Never questioning that woman, the voice from a few doors down simply smiles and nods at her every word while she darts back and forth from the poles of her anxiety. Perhaps the voice from a few doors down knows she needs tolerance and love before understanding can be had.

Whenever there is a meeting of all the voices, no one sits next to or even near that woman. Not even the voice from a few doors down. She simply plops herself in a chair and smiles at the room, as if she were a queen bee of sorts. At the last Christmas party, that woman resorted to reading tarot cards so that other voices would pay attention to her, but that did not work. In fact, another woman voice asked her if it could tell her fortune by reading her palm. After studying her hand for several seconds, the other woman voice announced jokingly: "Practice self-control and stop picking your nose." Well, that did it. The unsettled woman scooped up her tarot cards and flung them past her drooping, bottom lip to the floor.

Today the voice from a few doors down, now sprouting the wings of a worker bee, understands that its doorway is the best possible place to build a hive. The worker bee's on-cue laughing will nurture itself inside the hive. Then the doorway will close and that uneasy woman will have nowhere to go. She will spend the rest of her days running from doorway to doorway, fretting and wondering what happened to the voice from a few doors down. She will spread her tarot cards on the carpet in front of all doorways desperately seeking answers. More and more voices will walk around or look right through the perplexed woman. The honey bees will have moved on to another hive. And the voice from a few doors down will be in a faraway doorway hiding its spontaneity in the most unlikely of places.

Coin Game

"You know, just like real life."

The voice up front is outside and walking towards the back laneway to the parking lot. There it sees five different hands holding, then dropping or pointing to coins in the dirt.

The first hand is attached to a short, slender white arm and looks more like the paw of a dog; the voice up front imagines the hand being tied to a leash. It remains clenched for fear of losing its remaining coins. Or perhaps it is only an intruding dog paw wanting to push aside all hands and trot among the hands with no concern for coins. Something makes this first hand hesitate as it freezes outside the cluster of other hands.

The second hand belongs to a long, thick arm. This hand has already dropped a single coin on the ground and knows how to let go of anything; this makes the voice up front exhale slowly while watching. Its fingers, so long and thin that they seem to have no joints, are extended in a casual kind of way, as if the coin is a weight it carries around all day. The thumb on this hand is so long and thin that it seems out of place. And the rest of the fingers appear malnourished because the joints show nothing but raw bone.

The third hand, bent to the left of its wrist, casually drops the last coin in its grasp. Its wrist is small-boned and the distance to its elbow is short. The forearm glistens with sweat in the afternoon sunlight and almost blinds the voice up front.

Because it is losing interest in the coins, this hand may want to be somewhere else.

The fourth hand is huge, almost floppy, and may belong to someone whose skin grows faster than its bones. Its size makes the voice up front examine carefully its own hands. From the knuckles to the wrist, the back of this fourth hand is a hump, slowly finger-flicking itself away from the coin it left on the ground. Fading teeth-marks on the wrist are still red from a possible bracelet or wristwatch taken off not long ago, perhaps to bring the hand luck.

The fifth hand squeezes its coin until its fingers turn red then white. The voice up front sees the coin sticking out from a clenched fist that looks like the mouth of a puppet and the coin is a tongue speaking its own words. This makes the voice up front move closer until the hand moves away from the center of the coin game.

"This is my last coin," the fifth hand's voice trails off as it leaves the back laneway.

When the voice up front clears its throat, the other four hands ask it to join the game.

"How is it played?" the voice up front inquires.

"Take one coin from your pocket and hold it in your hand," answers the second hand.

"Done," replies the voice up front, reaching into its pocket and grasping a quarter.

"Now, flip the coin into the air and call 'heads' or 'tails'. Let it fall to the ground," the third hand says. "If your call is right, you keep all the coins in the dirt. If your call is wrong, you leave the coin in the dirt."

"Then what?" asks the voice up front.

"We keep flipping. The last one to make the correct call gets to keep all the remaining coins," the first hand says.

"Sooner or later, a wrong call is made," the fourth hand replies "Eventually someone runs out of coins and leaves. You know... just like real life."

October Leaf

"AND I DON'T WANT TO LOSE HIM, LIKE THAT FINAL LEAF FROM an October tree," she says.

The woman in the doorway has eyes that grow wider as they stare at the voice up front. Then her eyes dart from side to side, almost frantic, like wanting-to-talk eyes.

Later, when the room has emptied, she checks over both shoulders and approaches the voice up front.

"You once worked with my oldest son, Jack. Can we have a chat?"

"Sure. Have a seat," says the voice up front.

"Jack is unfinished," the woman says.

"What do you mean?"

"He joined the military and just left for the Middle East. He is only nineteen and not a big talker."

"Yes, I remember."

"Maybe I have the usual single mother concerns. When I stopped hugging him before he left, Jack asked me to start up his beat-up motorcycle every Friday so the engine got turned over regularly."

"That should help," says the voice up front. "Maybe that motorcycle will keep you both connected."

"Yeah, but my own engine needs turning over too," she replies hunching her shoulders. "Something tells me that my son is not done, that maybe he'll never be done."

"Why do you say that?"

"It's like he's a partially finished product and there's nothing I can do to complete him."

"Do you mean 'maturing'?"

"No, no. I realize he is still a boy in a man's skin. And I know it takes much longer for people to grow up today," she says.

"For sure. I read something recently that the parameters of adolescence used to be between twelve and eighteen and that now that can be between twelve and at least thirty or more. Seems that it has a lot to do with people being too dependent on other people, places and things and that these same people then start demanding that their needs be met, like children."

"No, I think the war will take care of that. It is much more."

"So what part of Jack needs to be finished?"

"He gets drained by being around people too much. Jack is a big-time introvert and completely stops talking every autumn," says the woman.

"How come?"

"He says he becomes like the last leaf on an October tree branch."

"Really?"

"Yes. And he does not speak to anyone until springtime when the tree buds start sprouting."

"How can he survive in the military? Surely, he needs to do some talking," the voice up front says, its face creased with question marks.

"Jack carries a pad of paper and writes notes to people saying that he has temporary vocal cord problems," the woman says.

"That's incredible," the voice up front replies. "And the army still recruited him."

Outside, the night time wind howls through mostly naked trees, its wailing so insistent that the only two people in this room have no choice but to show more compassion and understanding.

"And I don't want to lose him, like that final leaf from an October tree," she says.

Suddenly Saw

"I SUDDENLY SAW MY UNCLE CURLED UP, LIKE AN UNBORN something, on the bottom of a booze bottle and I wanted him born like before."

The voice up front looks up, his mouth like a cavern, at the tall, reed-like girl whose reddish hair hangs as strands of licorice. On her face is an earnestness that says that she wants to plant herself right here, right now. At first, she hesitates as she waves at the warm air coming from the ceiling vent. Then she asks the voice up front if it has time to talk.

"Sure," replies the voice up front. "What's going on?"

"Last week my uncle's right arm was handcuffed to a radiator by a family friend who is also a church minister. My uncle drinks so much that he may have developed a wet brain and forgot who he was. The minister brought him back to the church and put him in a small bedroom in the rectory. There he locked my uncle to a radiator next to the bed for five days."

"Handcuffed?"

All at once, there is a long, long pause in the room, as if the sun were both rising and catching its breath at the same time.

"The first couple of days my uncle tossed and turned and pleaded for more booze. All the minister did was check the handcuffs each time. On the second morning, my uncle was heard praying to the radiator for relief while sweating through his clothes. It was awful. The minister told my aunt that he stunk like a rotting corpse.

"What about feeding him and using the washroom?" asks the voice up front.

"Kept it simple with a spoon and a bowl. The only time he unlocked the handcuffs was when my uncle went to the washroom while the minister stood guard outside the door," the girl replies.

"That minister's got guts."

"For sure. On the third day my uncle started seeing animals like rats, a moose and a hippopotamus bursting out of the walls."

"Hallucinating?"

"That's what the minister said."

"That minister knows the truth."

"On the fourth day, my uncle stopped mumbling with spit dribbling down his chin so the minister allowed him to take a shower."

"Sounds like you were there too."

"Felt like it. My aunt called my mother twice a day with the latest. I was secretly listening on the other line," the girl says her head tipping to her chest, as if she were almost caught cheating at something.

"But what did all this listening do to you?" asks the voice up front.

"I used to take a bath every second day. Now two showers a day," the girl replies.

"How come?"

"I could smell my uncle when my aunt called and described it all. I vomited a couple of times when I first what was happening."

" It might have something to do with memory and how smell brings back the past."

"I suddenly saw my uncle curled up, like an unborn something, on the bottom of a booze bottle and I wanted him born like before."

Dolls

"MY MOTHER HAS MORE THAN ENOUGH ON HER SHOULDERS."

"Grandma gave me these porcelain dolls. She has no granddaughters," the boy with the acne-scarred face exclaims to the voice up front.

"So... what are your plans for the dolls?" the voice up front asks.

Just then, a girl standing nearby with eyeglasses that might belong to a near-sighted, secret spy, explodes with laughter.

"What's so funny?" asks the voice up front.

"What is he going to do with the dolls," the girl says with a smirk.

"The possibilities are endless," the voice up front replies. "Remember, these dolls are porcelain. They are probably worth something."

"My grandma has no other grandkids. She thinks I can sell them later and make some good money. I keep them in an old trunk in the basement. My mom hates dolls," the boy says.

"Why is that?" the voice up front asks.

"My mom says she is a grown-up woman. Also, when she was a little girl, her parents did not give her any pretty dolls. They told her that to be pretty is to be vain. Whenever my mom received a doll as a present from someone else, she would wait until that person left. Then she ripped off the doll's head, arms and legs to get rid of any vanity thoughts."

"Do you think that's true?" asks the voice up front. "About vanity?"

"No. If someone wants to look nice it does not mean that they are vain. Nothing wrong with looking good."

"Right. Nothing odd about that. Not at all. Do those porcelain dolls look like those Barbie Dolls?"

"Oh, yeah. I remember Barbie Dolls. Saw them on old TV shows. No... mine are heavier, taller. Not much of a shape to them. None of them are blondes or brunettes. Most are bald. Not too much pride with these porcelain dolls. They just lie there in the trunk, their rock-hard, white, white skin wrapped in plastic. No smiles. None."

"Does your mother ever... laugh?"

"I once saw a grin on her face when she was napping on the couch."

"How much do you think those dolls are worth?" inquires the voice up front.

"My dad has a friend who is an avid collector of things like hockey cards and goes to flea markets once a week. He will find out for me."

"How does someone put a price tag on a doll's head."

"Right. One week they are tossed aside and the next they are collectibles or maybe dropped into a trunk," the boy says with a partial laugh.

"What is it about dolls anyway?" the voice up front asks, his voice gentle but curious.

"I don't know but my grandma's dolls are nearly a hundred years old."

"Wow! I wonder how well dolls age?" asks the voice up front.

"Depends. My dolls seem to know how to stop time but, please... do not ask my mother."

"Why's that?"

"My mother has more than enough on her shoulders," says the boy.

Sidewalk

Lumbering down the weathered marble steps, they descend to sidewalk chattering.

One boy wearing blue jeans and a white turtleneck, paces back and forth unsure if the sidewalk is the only place for him. Then, suddenly back up the steps against the railing with a folder in his right hand, the same boy stands before the clogged doorway, as if this place has a hold on him or maybe he has forgotten something upstairs.

The voice up front forever encourages this same boy because the kid lights up when encouraged and is liked by everyone including all the other voices up front. Only the huge resident browbeater sees this boy as a target, but the bully is careful to only try something when the boy is completely alone, which is rare. And today at the open doorway, taunting thoughts pour out from the bully's ears onto the steps because the boy in the blue jeans tells the bully that if he ever needs help, he will be there for him, as if charming a bully solves everything.

A girl with long stringy hair the colour of fresh soil and wearing drywall-white slacks with large black polka dots and a black-as-night blouse, holds three books to her chest with both of her hands. She is in a hurry to leave as if her other home might be the sidewalk. Or perhaps she waits for someone near the bottom step. The calmness, the patience on her face is enough to teach everyone on the steps how to breathe themselves free from adolescence. And the books she embraces may contain irreplaceable words that are too much to share with the rest of the world.

A second boy carries a brand new, brown briefcase that swings back and forth in front of his right leg. Dressed in grey slacks and a thick navy sweater, too warm for this time of the year, he inhales the sunlight. In his left hand is a cigarette which he lit by the time his right foot hit the last step. This boy holds the lit cigarette at an arm's length from his mouth until he reaches the sidewalk and then inhales the length away from his smoke. The relief on his face is almost enough to make him stop and fling his briefcase in a half-circle up into the light of the sun.

Still another boy already planted on the sidewalk, wears khaki pants, shiny black loafers and a white T-shirt. Under his left arm he carries one of those zippered, black plastic sleeves bursting with books and paper. This boy is on a mission and if it were not for what was under his arm, he would be swinging his arms and marching like a soldier on manoeuvres. Not long ago the voice up front found out that this boy was in army cadets and trudging his way up the ranks.

A short-haired girl dressed in brand new dark blue jeans and a yellow blouse holds two books under her left arm against her rib cage. Her arms are held apart at her elbows and an enormous smile forces her cheeks up to her eyes. She welcomes the afternoon sun on her face and prepares to cross the road right there instead of using the cross-walk down the street. Amazingly, drivers do not run her over because they are too busy stopping and waving. Her smile can direct any traffic and the voice up front once suggested that she bottle what she had and sell it in pharmacies.

Out comes the voice up front with its briefcase stuffed with so much paper that the briefcase might be growing ears. Suddenly halting and sitting on the bottom step over to the left, the voice up front plops its briefcase between its legs. Bodies of all shapes and sizes navigate around the voice up front, some nearly tripping and several with looks of surprise. When asked by another voice up front what it was doing sitting on the front step like that, the voice up front replies: "Just for now, my voice is practicing the art of saying very little."

ABOUT THE AUTHOR

Photo by Frank O'Donnell

BORN AND RAISED IN MONTREAL, KEN RIVARD HOLDS A
Master's Degree from McGill University. Including UP
FRONT, Ken has published 12 books professionally in various genres including: flash/postcard fiction, poetry, children's
literature and the novel. Ken's 11th book, a substantial collection of flash fiction entitled CANALWATCH was published
by Mosaic Press in Spring, 2022. His writing has appeared in
numerous anthologies, in many regional and national pub-
lications and on CBC Radio. Ken's books have been final-
ists for the Writers Guild of Alberta Book Awards including
the City of Calgary W.O. Mitchell Book Prize. In 2015, his
novel, MOTHERWILD (2014) was longlisted for Canada's
ReLit Book Award. Ken has presented numerous readings

and workshops across Canada and has served as a writing mentor in 2017-2018 for the Writers Guild of Alberta Writing Mentorship Program. He has worked as a juror for the Writers Union of Canada and for both the Alberta and Saskatchewan Book Awards. In addition, Ken has been the Writer-in-Residence for both the Calgary Public Library and the Writers Guild of Alberta (Strawberry Creek). For many years he has been living and writing in Calgary. His website can be found at: kenrivard.ca.